A Dawlish Maid

By Roma Dillon-Everest

Acknowledgements

"Many thanks to my dear husband, Tony, who helped 'behind the scenes' whilst I was writing this book"

"Also, thanks to Sara Williams, Rob Young, Sheila Coates, Jacki Coe, Tom Hunt, Alan Mobbs, Val & Mike Wedlake, Janet Hunt, Josephine Hill and Brian Steffens for their advice"

First Published September 2023

ISBN 978-1-3999-6725-9

CHAPTER ONE

It was the night of the Dawlish pantomime rehearsal, which was being held at the Hut, Georgina being only seven years old at the time, was very proud to be a ballet dancer in the production of 'Puss in Boots'. It was also the night when the news of a dangerous prisoner having escaped from the high security jail at Dartmoor Prison which was only about 30 miles away. Michael, Georgina's older brother had been instructed by their mother and father to walk Georgina home, he decided to hurry his younger sister out of the wooden building and get her home as quickly as possible. Michael secretly had another reason to get home early, he was missing the final episode of Quatermass and the Pit! For a 21 year old lad that was really worth seeing.

Little did they realise that they were not alone when hurrying past the old orchard in Elm Grove Road. On the other side of the hedge, a tall, well built ugly brute of a man was lying under a piece of corrugated iron that he had found, another piece he had laid down to act as a floor which made a makeshift shelter up against the thickest part of the hedge. He was freezing cold. The Crombie coat, that he had stolen from the prison guard that he had killed, was sodden. He pulled the collar up around his ears, his dark greasy strands of hair appeared to be stuck to his head, he folded his arms and tried to sleep.

His journey from the prison was cold but he kept moving. He had a good couple of hours ahead of the search party. The Warder, that he had killed, was in the gardening shed alone. Prisoner 1852 had been a model inmate and had been given 'special duties' status, so was put to work in the gardening party. His good behaviour was all part of his plan to keep his eyes open and wait for the right time to make his escape. He had attended several training schemes, that the prison had offered, in readiness for his return, if ever, to life outside the prison walls. He had learnt to read and write, successfully been on a basic plumbing course and was learning building and carpentry skills. A report about him from a prison doctor was that he was an intelligent man who needed to keep his brain active.

Unfortunately, his terrible upbringing had affected his outlook on life. He had become exceptionally selfish, he was cruel to other inmates, at all times, given the opportunity. He was a psychopath, he had abnormal violent tendencies and could not be trusted. Socially, he was able to get what he wanted through lying, conning and manipulating people then winning them over.

His opportunity came when he managed to steal a six inch knife as he delivered, to the kitchens, a sack of potatoes that he had dug up alongside other

4

inmates a few months before and were stored in a garden shed. When

he returned to the shed the radio was loudly playing the latest pop song, he

crept silently up behind his prey then slashed the Warder's throat with ease,

the prisoner heard the blood gurgle in his victim's throat – that was the only

sound. He let the body slump to the floor quietly. There was no-one around

so he put on the man's Prison Service hat and coat then jumped over the small

wall surrounding the gardens.

He only had to walk on the road for a few minutes, the thick mist was

not moving around and visibility was very poor, he was then able to get out

onto the inhospitable moor without being seen. He swiftly went uphill and

over the top of the tor.

It wasn't long before the winter's night closed in. He stayed just over the

ridge of the tors so that he could follow the few car lights on the winding road

leading off the moor as much as possible. The escapee tried to avoid the

boggy areas on the moor but found that quite a difficult task as the light faded,

so after a few miles over the uneven boggy ground, with the drizzly fine rain

blowing into his face, he was soaking wet up to his knees and wanted to stop

for a short rest, but he knew he mustn't, the dogs would be deployed soon if

not already.

He kept thinking that he used to look at the moor through the bars and

glass of his cell and always admired the beauty of the tors, the changing

seasons making them look stunning. Even on misty days the views were magical.

Now, as he was spending a very cold night on the moor he had changed
his mind and cursed the English weather. He eventually hid in a crack on the
leeward side of an outcrop of granite boulders, having picked a large amount
of dead bracken to make a sort of mattress. At first light he decided to start
walking again through the boggy ground. He needed an early start – he was
getting very cold – he needed to keep moving.

Avoiding all roads he was covered in mud when he reached Bovey
Tracey. He found the park beside the river and walked through it, he then
crossed the lane and made his way through the woodland still following the
river upstream. Keeping out of sight of the dog walkers, he managed to have
a quick wash and clean his very muddy boots. He used handfuls of dock
leaves to try to get the mud from his trousers and was satisfied that he didn't
look quite as bad as before.

Keeping to the woods and fields again he reached Chudleigh Knighton.
The small Post Office was open. Outside the shop, the owner had put some
apples and oranges on display. Prisoner 1852 helped himself, then quickly
walked down the path and disappeared into the small copse that ran beside the
road. The oranges and apples were enjoyed quickly, both being large, sweet
and juicy.

He heard a police car coming his way as he was heading out of the
woodland and into the field. Instead of going up the Teign Valley he decided

to head towards Chudleigh then realised he had made a mistake. The children were going to school, farmers were moving sheep or going from field to field by tractor - there were lots of people going about their business. Looking across the valley he saw a police car heading towards Chudleigh Knighton – he sniggered to himself that he had stayed one step ahead of the police.

He stayed for a quick rest under an old bridge by a stream. No one could see him hiding, there were no houses nearby but the threat of the police finding him was strong and he knew, if he was caught, he would certainly be imprisoned for the rest of his life.

There didn't seem to be anyone about on this stretch of road, so he left the bridge and quickly managed to get into an empty field, he then followed the hedge up the long hill. There was a big house across the road and, just as he was looking through the thick vegetation that surrounded the field, a middle-aged well-dressed couple came out of the house, the man drove their expensive looking modern car through the gate, the woman closed it then she got into the car. As soon as they had driven up the hill and out of sight, the prisoner pushed his way through the hedge, ran across the road and made his way into the garden.

He was in luck, no-one was around and the small downstairs toilet window had been left open. He went into the garden shed, found some tools, which he thought he may need and using all of his skills that he had learnt when making his living as a burglar, he clambered into the house taking care to wipe the window sill clean of the mark from his boot, he then made his way first to the sitting room, then the study, then up to the main bedroom. He looked into all the usual hiding places for money or nice pieces of jewellery. He found the money, £20, in a small purse in a handbag in the wardrobe.

"That will do nicely" he muttered to himself.

He still had a few ideas of where valuables could be stashed and continued his search. After a few minutes he hit the jackpot. Under the dressing table a small cotton bag was taped to the underpart of the bottom drawer. He opened it eagerly and found four exquisite well cut gems. He hastily put the small pouch in his pocket and before making his way to the door, he rummaged through the wardrobe and put a pair of trousers, a thick jumper, a scarf, gloves, a couple of shirts, several pairs of socks and some underwear on the bed then wrapped them up in a blanket and put them into a medium sized valise that he had found in a cupboard. He then went to the bathroom and helped himself to a razor, a packet of razor blades, a small shaving mirror, a bar of soap and a towel.

He made his way down the stairs then, as he was heading for the back door, he noticed the larder door and saw, to his delight, a hanging meat safe with a still warm plump cooked chicken inside, it smelt delicious, he wrapped it in a tea towel and placed that into the valise with a bottle of whisky that was on the kitchen dresser. A fruit cake and all the fruit that was in the fruit bowl was put into the bag as well. He loved any fruit, probably because he never ate one until he was about 13 years old.

Within minutes he was back into the field and heading uphill. He carried on walking from field to woodland following the lane. Eventually he came to Ashcombe Church, it was now getting dark and he needed to sleep. Turning right at the bottom of the hill and passing a few cottages, he came to a track on the right, this he followed up a very steep hill and eventually came to a tumble-down barn and thought it would do for the night.

He was starving hungry so, after taking off his wet clothes and putting on the stolen trousers, one of the shirts, the jumper and warm socks, he wrapped the blanket around him and settled down to eat. He fell asleep soon after eating, he didn't go into a deep sleep, he needed to stay alert.

The next morning he was awake before it was light. Making his way down the very steep hill, he found a stream and decided, after looking around, to slosh some water over his face. He would find somewhere less open to have a shave. It wasn't long before he found a small copse with a stream flowing through it. He felt so much better after getting rid of the stubble on his face.

The signpost pointed to Dawlish one way and Starcross the other. He had heard of Dawlish and knew they had a railway station, but that lane was very busy with people going to work, so he decided to go the other way.

It wasn't long before the lane divided, then divided again with no signposts. Prisoner 1852 was completely lost. He kept walking feeling quite tired again and the leather valise seemed to be very heavy. He had money in his pocket and some priceless jewels, warm clothes and a blanket, he still had half of the chicken left which was wrapped in the tea towel and his dirty, sweaty prison shirt.

After going down a long steep hill he came to a farm, he then turned right then left. He came across a small, old corrugated iron building. He was looking for somewhere to sleep that night, but there were no sides to this building and he could have been seen by anyone from the road, the farmhouse or the red brick cottage at the edge of the wood on the other side of the field. He decided to carry on.

One hundred yards up the lane, the road opened out and he was looking at a collection of red brick houses surrounding a lawn with a massive oak tree in the middle. According to the sign in the garden of number 60 it was called Newlands.

He continued his journey which led him to the main road. He turned right and after about 100 yards, to his horror he saw, in the distance, a police road block. He quickly turned around, he was so quick he realised that they hadn't seen him. He made his way back to Elm Grove Road and went as fast as he could up the now dark road. Following the long high wall of the market garden he saw, in the dim moonlight, a small orchard. The gate was old and partly broken and the weeds in front of the gate were quite high. It suggested that no-one had gone in there for quite a while, so he trod carefully aiming to step close to the bottom of the wall so the weeds were not disturbed.

He found two pieces of corrugated iron and made a shelter. The wind started to howl through the trees and the rain was getting heavier. He was now so cold and tired, he ate the last of the chicken and drank the last of the whisky, wrapped the blanket around him and slept deeply.

CHAPTER TWO

It was two years since Georgina's father died and she missed him terribly. The family that she belonged to was large and happy, her older brother and sisters were all married and had left home for a life with their own families.

One day she came home from school, her mother made a pot of tea and sat at the table with her - Georgina knew she had something to say.

It wasn't long before she said "I am afraid I won't be able to let you go on the secretarial course at Torquay Technical College, now that your dad has died I can't afford it".

That was a bitter blow to Georgina, she had always dreamt of being 'an important person's private secretary'. Blinking through the tears she decided this dream would have to go on the back burner!

Hiding her disappointment she said "Don't worry Mum, I will go and get a job".

She rushed into her bedroom and cried for what seemed like hours, then thought 'Dad would be proud of me if I made my dreams come true and one day I will. I will become an exceptionally good secretary'.

New clothes were the only thing she had to go without. He mother was never a follower of fashion, probably due to the fact that she brought up three children in London during the war and only had clothes coupons and parcels from America to clothe herself, the ever growing Michael, Mary, and baby Eileen. Their father was a Military Policeman in the Army so was abroad most of the six years of war. Georgina knew they were bombed out during the blitz and although that was terrible it resulted in her mum sending Michael and Mary to Dawlish as evacuees – as far as Georgina was concerned that was the only good thing that had come out of that dreadful war!

One winter night, when she was about seven years old, she had been a ballet dancer in a Dawlish pantomime rehearsal at the Hut, Michael, who was then twenty one years old, was told by his Mum and Dad to meet Georgina then walk her home. He was angry at this because he felt he would miss the last episode of Quatermass on the television. To make matters worse, when they walked along the Exeter Road they came across a police roadblock at the top of Iddesleigh Terrace. They shone a torch in his face and asked a lot of questions as to why Georgina was out that late. There had been a jail break at Dartmoor prison and a violent prisoner was running loose. As soon as they turned into the very dark Elm Grove Road, there were no street lights or pavements till the bottom of Newlands, Michael seemed to walk a lot faster which Georgina found very frightening, but he knew that a lot of the prisoners from Dartmoor were very dangerous and he wanted to get home, with Georgina, as quickly as possible.

It was a dark winter's night and the high wind in the many trees were blowing strongly, constantly shedding everywhere any leaves that were left after the autumnal winds. The mist and drizzle made the smaller trees seem creepy and the twisting small branches made eerie noises as they rubbed together in the wind. Georgina wanted to cry, she found it difficult to keep pace with Michael even though he was pushing their sister Eileen's bike with his right hand and gripping tightly to the hand of his younger sister with the other. The wind was relentless and very noisy.

The thought of a prisoner from any prison hiding in the hedges down this spooky road scared her against the dark for the rest of her life.

As she got older Georgina found going anywhere by bike was really fun, but there was always an element of danger. One day she was riding down Elm Grove Road, the sun was shining and there were a few people about. She rode down to post a letter at Oak Park Road for her mum. As she stopped to put the envelope in the box, she was startled to see a man who was standing across the road slowly pull his raincoat apart and exposed himself, his mouth curled up into a self-satisfied grin. Georgina was so shocked, she had never seen a man do that before and she knew it was naughty so she got on her bike and rode home as quickly as she could. Her mum was in the garden when she arrived, Georgina was shaken and distressed and started to cry when she told her story. Her mum was really quite angry, she left Georgina with her sister Eileen and ran down the road. It wasn't long before she came back and told Eileen that he had disappeared. Georgina's dad was even angrier when he came home from work. He asked her a lot of questions as to the man's appearance and all Georgina could say was that he was very ugly.

"I will have a word with Sergeant Stevens tomorrow" Georgina's father said. "Meanwhile, do try to forget this happened but just remember not to speak to strangers".

He then carried her up the stairs, gave her Pandy to cuddle and kissed her goodnight as he tucked her into bed. He knew that Pandy, the cuddly soft Panda given to her by her godmother at her christening, would settle her down. It had always worked when she was poorly.

*   *   *   *   *

Georgina was looking forward to her tenth birthday in a few days. It was a misty, warm morning during the six week summer holiday from school but was not a beach day so Georgina and her friends from Newlands spent the day playing on the green. Her Auntie and Uncle and cousin Patsy were coming to stay for their annual holiday by the sea. When Georgina saw their taxi arrive she rushed to greet her family from London.

After tea, Auntie Ruth came downstairs with a brown carrier bag full of clothes that Patsy had outgrown. This was like Christmas to Georgina – she loved these dresses they were always so pretty. Georgina couldn't wait to try them on, most fitted her well, some had to go into the cupboard until next summer, but she was delighted. One dress she particular liked was a dark blue cotton one with a very tiny floral design and two large patch pockets - Georgina fell in love with it.

"Can I wear this one tomorrow mum, it's so lovely?" Georgina asked.

The following day Georgina skipped, in her new dark blue dress, up to the green to meet with her friends who were already there. They started to walk down the lane towards the old market. This building was barely the size of a couple of sheds and made of corrugated iron sheets, it was situated at the edge of the wood and belonged to the farmer at Gatehouse farm. They all climbed the gate and got into the field.

"Let's play pom-pom" said Leonard.

The children had been taught this game by the generation before them. In other areas it was called 'hide and seek'.

Leonard decided to be the hunter and hid his eyes, he then started counting 5, 10, 15, 20 ...... Everyone scattered. Most of the children headed to the corner of the field where they climbed the hedge and bank into the farmer's wood. For some reason Georgina decided to go back to the lane then realised she had nowhere to go.

The field at the back of Newlands was in the process of being ploughed by the farmer's eldest son, she knew he would be along shortly so her only option was to go into Mr Healy's wood, but no-one ever went in there because it was said that, if found by Mr Healy he would shoot you that's if the aliens didn't get you from the crater that was made when a meteorite crash landed in the woods!

Suddenly she heard Leonard shouting "100 coming ready or not".

Without thinking she quickly squeezed herself through the beech hedge and over the boundary bank – she was in the wood, alone!

Leonard must have been peeping because he immediately started to run towards the corner of the field where the other children had gone. So with him out of earshot Georgina managed to go further into the wood. She was very scared of being shot so she crept through the undergrowth as quietly as she could.

Suddenly she heard twigs breaking, her heart was thumping and her brain was telling her to hide. 'Hide while you can' it said, 'Climb up a tree, don't go further into the wood, you will bump into Mr Healy, or worse still, you will bump into the aliens from the meteorite who were probably like the giant grasshopper creatures in Quatermass'.

Georgina was close to tears. She saw an old fir tree which looked easy to climb and shinned up there faster than she ever thought possible. It was easy and so within seconds she found that she could see the corner of the field – it looked as though the boys and girls were coming back. They could outrun Leonard and did so. By this time Georgina was balancing with two legs on one branch and holding on for dear life to the smaller branch above it. Her legs were uncontrollably shaking she was so scared.

The noise of the twigs breaking came to a stop and Georgina managed to look down and saw a man standing under the tree – her tree. She recognised him straight away – it was the ugly man who had shown his private parts to her. She was frozen to the tree and started to tremble, her hands were clinging onto the branch so tightly that they were numb – she had no control over them.

He started to move towards the lane and was counting his strides, then when he got to ten beside a large boulder, he bent down and dug a hole then put a small bag inside, he covered the hole with earth, twigs, leaves and pine needles. She then noticed that he had a tattoo of a snake coiling around an anchor on his right arm. Georgina felt that she was going to lose her grip but she knew she must not fall. The man walked towards the lane then went through the hedge on top of the bank. Georgina could see him through the branches of the broad leaved trees he then disappeared up the lane towards Newlands.

"I still haven't found Georgina yet, where did she go?" asked Leonard. Nobody seemed to know.

"I don't think she would have gone into the wood on her own, I think she has gone home. I am getting hungry now so I am going home as well, see you all later" said Mitch.

All the children decided that was a good idea so they all went home for dinner.

Georgina wanted desperately to join them and tried to shout but no sound was coming from her mouth. Eventually she was able to climb down the fir tree and, against the warnings of her conscience, she crept over to where the covered hole was, found it, put her hand in and felt a cotton bag. There were some really pretty stones in there, two red ones, one green and one blue.

'Oh, they are really pretty, I am going to take them home' she thought.

She put the stones in the pocket of her new dress, then re-buried the bag. While still creeping nearly on tip-toes in the wood she came to the hedge then quickly pushed her way through again. She felt relieved to be out of the wood and promised herself she would never go in there again, she was also so happy with what she had found and started to skip up the lane but, the ugly man she had just seen in the wood was sitting on the wall at the bottom of Newlands which made her nervous again even though there were plenty of people around. Mr Cribb was trimming his hedge surrounding his garden and her aunt Lully was chatting to Leonard's mum at the end of her garden path.

Georgina's legs were shaking again but she managed to wave to her aunt, ignore the man and somehow ran indoors without even looking at him. He could tell she was the same little girl he flashed to because she couldn't look at him, there was something odd about her seeing him. It was more than the flash – it was as if she felt guilty about something. The idea that she had the jewels never entered his head on this day.

She didn't want to tell her mum about the stones because she was in the wood and had been told repeatedly not to go in there, she knew she would get into trouble for disobeying her, so she ran upstairs and decided the hide the stones. She was too young to realise their worth but she thought they were too pretty to part with them. It was looking at Pandy, the soft toy panda, that made up her mind. He had a small split between the black and the now off-white material by his right arm so she pushed the stones through that and thought she would sew it up another day. She then went downstairs for her dinner.

CHAPTER THREE

Several years later when Georgina was 16, Michael's wife, Steph, was taken to the Exeter hospital and came home with a beautiful baby girl, who looked very much like her mother, having the same dark hair and pretty features. Michael insisted that any daughter of his would be given a boy's name so his elder daughter Jacqueline would be known as Jack or Jackie, now their new-born would be called Lesley.

The family made sure that the baby's head was wetted in accordance with family tradition at the Swan Inn, the oldest pub in Dawlish, where there was always a big welcoming open fire glowing in the bar on winter nights and this mid-January night was no exception.

Michael was very popular because of his wonderful sense of humour and the family, being local, were well known and were joined in the lounge of the inn by lots of local people. Their sister Mary, her husband George and son Alan were already there. So when John and Eileen arrived with their daughters Karen and Wendy, the family were altogether.

During the celebration Georgina knew most of the local lads who were there from school days, but one in particular caught her eye. Although he was a year older than her, she couldn't really remember him at school, but when he came over to her table she noticed just how good looking he was. His dark hair and eyes, which were intently focusing on her, really excited the sixteen year old naïve young girl.

"Hello Maid, how are you getting on, haven't seen you for ages?" he said as he put his pint of beer down on the table in front of her he met her gaze with his deep brown piercing eyes. He added "Would you like a drink?"

Although she was very conscious of the fact that she should not have been in the pub because of her age, and knowing that he shouldn't have been there as well because of the same reason, she wondered if she could, at least try, to sound experienced, knowledgeable and grown up.

"Can I have a gin and orange please Matt" she said while tucking a loose strand of her light brown hair behind her ear.

Hoping that she sounded more of a modern girl about town than the naïve young girl that she really was, she watched him walk up to the bar and noticed his athletic build, it was her first taste of admiring a member of the opposite sex. When he came back to the table she offered him a cigarette, which he accepted and they laughed and joked until their sides ached even though they were surrounded by lots of noisy chatter from the crowded pub.

Before the 'Last Orders' bell had been rung her mother had sorted out a lift home. An old family friend drove his two seater pick-up truck at a very slow speed to take them home with Georgina and her mother being squashed in the passenger seat. Georgina's mother was only being protective towards her and she was very polite to Matt, but she managed to get her daughter into the truck before she realised what was happening.

Unfortunately, Georgina thought, nothing came of this liaison at this time, but Georgina did learn about that funny feeling deep inside your tummy that you get sometimes when just talking to the opposite sex. Goodness, she was so excited, so naïve and so completely smitten!!

*   *   *   *   *

Life in the small town of Dawlish returned to some sort of normality after all that excitement for quite some time.

It was really good to get out and walk along the beach on dry, windy winter days, Georgina took the family dog, Rusty, to Coryton Cove - the local's beach. The tide was beginning to turn and the gulls that had flocked together, were making their usual stress calls whilst scavenging as if they were either angry or hungry. The rock pools were full of small fish and tiny crabs, so the gulls were kept busy in their quest to find breakfast knowing that a bird next to them would steal their catch at the first opportunity.

Rusty bounded towards the birds making them fly above him trying to negotiate the North West wind which was blowing strongly and whipping up the surf to a high pinnacle of roaring white froth.

She was thrilled when Matt joined her, he must have seen her walking along the town beach. They ran round like a pair of school kids and finished up at the top of Lea Mount.

They slowly walked passed the two gun emplacements. The painted bottle green wooden seats inside were always wet from the rain blowing in and sitting there was never a good choice in the winter months. To get out of the wind they went behind the stone buildings, Matt wanted a cuddle, but it was just as cold there.

"Matt, it's freezing, let's keep walking" she said.

They carried on their walk to the old underground WWII arsenal at the top of the grassy area. The sloping pathway was dank, damp and smelly and it looked as if someone had tried to get in because the bottom of the old painted bottle green wooden door had been broken. This green paint was known locally as council house green. The colour of the doors and windows at Newlands were always bottle green as was the Avenues.

"Surely, someone wouldn't think there would still be ammunition in there now, Matt?"

"If they did, they would be in for a shock – it would all be really damp in there now" he replied.

Although it was winter, and the winds felt as if they were cutting a body in half, it didn't deter the passion that ran through their veins.

They found the little path that led to nowhere but during the war it led to the walking bridge that was used by the soldiers and the Home Guard to go to another gun emplacement across the road.

The path was now overgrown but they made their way through and lay down to rest their legs. Matt lay so that her head could rest in the crook of his arm, she felt tingly and warm when she snuggled into his strong muscular arms. She looked at him from that angle and found that he was looking at her. Their eyes met in an instant, he kissed her passionately.

CHAPTER FOUR

Several of Georgina's friends got engaged during the summer of 1966.
Her dear friend from the Catholic school, Christina, sent her a letter just saying
'come to my beach hut in Teignmouth I have some exciting news'. Georgina
caught the bus over – Christina, looking as lovely as ever, was ecstatic. It was a
non-stop smile from her as she explained that she was engaged to be married to
a local chap and, hopefully, they would be married in a couple of years.
Georgina was so pleased to see her friend so happy.

 The beach hut belonged to Christina's mum it was well kitted out
with all the things needed for a day at the beach. It was a simple eight foot by
six foot wooden hut but the location was stunning. It was right on the point at
Teignmouth, by the lighthouse, overlooking the river. It could not have been a
better day, plenty of warm sunshine and the view towards Shaldon was terrific.
They spent the whole day drinking tea and eating bacon sandwiches that
Christina made on the little primus stove and after that devouring slices of
ginger cake, that her mother had made, which was then packed up to take to the
beach. All talk was discussing lads in general, but the conversation was
obviously always going to be Christina's love, and Georgina was really pleased
that she was so happy.

 They had always been pair of gigglers and today was no exception, they laughed until they cried – it was really good therapy. Georgina suddenly looked at her watch and realised that the time had gone so quickly – she must hurry to get home and glam herself up to go to the dance tonight.

"We'll meet up again soon, Georgina" Christina said as she waved her friend goodbye.

On the journey home Georgina went into deep thoughts about her other two friends just recently engaged and seriously mulled over the fact that she didn't even have a boyfriend or, at least, not one in particular. Never mind, there's always my dream man – haven't seen him for ages, I wonder what he is up to – what a lovely bum he has!

Her thoughts soon got the better of her as she was roller coasting into visions of Lady Chatterley and Mellors deep in the woods. Thoughts of the wood reminded her of Mr Healy's wood. She quickly put the thoughts of the ugly man out of her head, he scared her now.

Her thoughts came to an end when she realised she was on the bus from Teignmouth and it was now at the Dawlish bus stop. She made her way home quickly because all the girls had planned on going to the local dance that evening and as Georgina was getting ready she tried to get herself into the right mood to attract Matt. 'Now which dress would he like best?' She was asking herself. 'I think he would prefer the blue and white one with the white collar with white sandals – that will be all I need, that and a bit of lippy should do it'. Her tan was looking good and after all the giggles this afternoon she felt on top of the world.

The local dance was not what they all had hoped for. There were not many people attending and there was a severe shortage of the opposite sex. Penny, who had been talking to a local lad at the other end of the bar, came over to say that Matt Thackery had just got engaged and we're all invited to his mum and dad's place for a party tonight!

Georgina grabbed hold of the bar, she thought she was going to faint. How could he! He's mine! Who is this girlfriend? How dare she! Why haven't I seen him with her? Georgina found she couldn't speak to the other girls – she was rocked to the core and it felt like she was so upset she couldn't even cry.

'How will I cope at his house, perhaps I should get drunk, throw my drink over her, or get her drunk'? All these thoughts were rattling around in Georgina's head. 'Why didn't he say he had a girlfriend when he last walked me home from the Gaiety Coffee Bar? Why did he egg me on? Why did he make me think I was special to him?'

The girls all linked arms and headed for the road in which he lived. Georgina had to go along with them. The girls had no idea she felt like that about him they wouldn't understand if she went all miserable on them or even feigned illness to try to get out of going to this party. She had no choice but to go.

When they got to the house his mother was there to let them in.

"Hello girls, in you come, oh! Hello Georgina, how nice to see you again

– haven't seen you since the baby's head wetting party. How is the new baby?"

"Doing very well thank you" replied Georgina.

She thought for a moment and wondered why his mum had singled her out – does she feel sorry for me?

Matt was over at the makeshift bar with a most striking looking girl and they were standing very close to one another, he was all over her like a rash!

'That must be her', Georgina thought. 'Oh my, I don't know what to do'.

Susan came over with two glasses in her hands. "Come on Georgina here's your drink, whatever is the matter? Looks like you've seen a ghost!" she said.

Georgina was barely able to speak she just mumbled "I feel sick".

She darted out of the room and into the garden managing somehow to keep the tears from rolling. She knew that her rival was so attractive she just couldn't compete. She started to feel sorry for herself.

'Why am I always being disappointed in life!' she wondered.

The party was in full swing, everyone having a good time. The Rolling Stones were blaring out their hits on the record player and two local lads, Ashley and Bob were throwing their arms about and trying to mimic Mick Jagger – it was hilarious!

Georgina was still out in the garden talking to anyone and everyone so long as she didn't have to talk to HER. The garden was beautiful, his mum and dad spent a lot of time making it look fabulous. The lawn had stripes and the flower beds were a riot of colour, but it still could not make Georgina feel better.

It seemed that Matt and this new girl were joined at the hip, he never left her side all the time Georgina was there. He never went anywhere near Georgina or even acknowledged her in any way. She was so upset by his callous behaviour she thought she would never get over it. A great cloud had come over her that was darkening by the minute.

'I can't cope with this I am going home. I will sneak out the back gate – nobody will notice I have gone – not even Matt' she thought miserably.

CHAPTER FIVE

Sitting on the lawn in Dawlish having lunch in the sunshine most working days was a real treat when one was cooped up all day in a shop in the summer months. The girls always envied the holidaymakers and watched them play with their children, eating their picnics or just sunbathing. The dads playing football with a soft ball for the toddlers and having to keep a watchful eye on them in case they toddled over to the stream where the black swans and ducks were - it all looked good fun.

Susan said "Why don't we go on holiday somewhere, September can be a nice month weather wise".

"That sounds like a good idea, can't go too far I wouldn't be able to afford it" said Georgina.

She also thought that to get away would be good for her instead of just pining away stuck in Dawlish for ever and a day - getting upset about Matt.

Laura chipped in "Let's all think about it over the weekend and put it to the vote Monday lunchtime. By the way, who is that man wandering around? He passed us just now, I don't know if you noticed him - he's not nice to look at. He was really staring at you Georgina – must be the man of your dreams ha, ha".

Georgina looked at him, she hadn't noticed him walking past at all, but she recognised him – he was that same ugly man from years ago!

"Man of my nightmares more like" said Georgina casually.

She sat quietly thinking about him – he was definitely the man who flashed at her and she felt certain he was the same man who was in the wood that day when they played pom-pom down at the old market. Georgina had no idea he was still around, she suddenly realised that he must want his stones back - why else would he still be hanging around. Her heart started thumping, she looked towards where he was and found that he had gone, she couldn't see him.

'How would he know I have the stones – I have never spoken to anyone about them' she thought.

She began to feel nervous and was thankful the girls were there, and was pleased when Susan said that it was time for them all to go back to work. As they stood to start the walk to the shop, Georgina noticed that he was behind them just staring at her. He quickly managed to get ahead of them then smiled eerily at Georgina when the girls passed him, his full set of yellowing misshapen teeth made her shudder. He never spoke – he just gave a sneering smile directly to her. He gave Georgina the creeps.

When Georgina walked to work on the following Monday, she was feeling very excited about her idea for the holiday to London and kept thinking about King's Road and Carnaby Street and couldn't wait to tell the girls about her idea for a break in September. She also thought she may get to see Simon, her cousin Paul's friend, she liked him a lot.

Her feelings of elation came crashing down when she turned the corner at the bottom of Strand Hill and saw the ugly man looking in Woolworth's shop window. Her nervousness was showing, the beads of sweat were trickling down the sides of her temples, her knees wobbled as she tried to hurry to get into the shop where she worked. She was heading for the side door, which was always kept unlocked for the staff. She managed to get in but she thought that he saw her as she was pushing the door closed. Georgina managed to click the lock into position and thought she would stay behind the door and let in the staff when they knocked.

One by one the staff came to the door and Georgina let them in. They all asked for an explanation and she just said that a chap was hanging around and she didn't like to leave the door unlocked, which was true. She didn't elaborate or explain that she had come across him before, she just hoped he would go away.

She decided to put on her overall and get into the shop when the last assistant had come in. Luckily the boss asked her to do some stocktaking so she was not in the shop all day.

"It's my turn to make coffee and tea this week, I will bring yours up to you" said Wendy.

"Thanks, Wendy".

The room where she had to do the stocktaking had a big window that overlooked the Strand, she had a quick peep but couldn't see the pavement or the front of the shop because of the sun blinds that had been pulled out that covered everything. Happily she saw the back of the ugly man walking through the Lawn heading towards the railway station. The only thing she had to worry about was going home, if he was around. She didn't want him to follow her and find out that she still lived at Newlands. She decided to feign illness at lunchtime then ask if she could go home early at about 4pm.

Wendy bought Georgina a cup of coffee at about 11 o'clock and, after thanking her, Georgina sat on the stool and looked out of the window. She was trying to find a way in her mind of avoiding the ugly man. She certainly didn't really want to go to the police, she thought that would be the last thing the ugly man would want her to do. Being so scared of him she didn't want to upset him, although he was spooky and weird he seemed to be quite approachable – but not by her – she was too nervous, but who could stand up to him?

The ugly man knew she had the stones, her reaction told him as soon as she noticed him the week before on the Lawn, he was not stupid.   He had been to check on the stones over the weekend, after he had seen her, when he found the stones had disappeared he knew it was her. Her guilt gave her away - her attitude and actions towards him were not normal.

When he saw that the stones had gone, there was just the empty bag left in the hole, he went berserk, he kicked the large boulder and started thumping the trees in his anger. He snapped every small branch that was lying around and smashed his way through the wood and out onto the lane.

"I will get that little bitch, if it's the last thing I ever do. Nobody will say that I, Robert, would be beaten by a ten year old. Little cow" he ranted.

He knew he would be really short of money at some stage, he knew he would have to either go back to burglary, of which he didn't want to do. He was caught last time and finished up in Dartmoor or he could terrorise this young girl, who he knew had 'his' jewels. He chose the latter.

Lust came over him. She had now matured into an attractive young woman and he wanted her above all others. He sensed that she was definitely frightened of him. He was powerful in every sense of the word, he knew that. He would have her at some stage, but at the moment he was having fun just turning up out of the blue and scaring her. He had power over her. It seemed to make it more of a 'cat and mouse' game and in his depraved way he was enjoying it.

*   *   *   *   *

Laura, Susan and Georgina were eager to get on the overnight coach to London for their holiday and they had a fabulous time. They visited all the sights and Georgina met up with Simon again. After seven tiring days and drinking for seven nights, the girls certainly had a ball.

But it had to end so the girls were on the coach heading back to Dawlish nursing headaches from the drinks the night before. They agreed that Susan's white jeans, that she had drawn different coloured triangles on, then wore to

Hampton Court, was a definite plus to the memory of the holiday. The jeans were so 'ahead of the fashion' that everybody stared in amazement and probably wanted a pair. Georgina tried to hide her anxiousness regarding going back to Dawlish, she was not looking forward to going home for fear of the ugly man following her, and he really scared her now.

'He must be after those stones, I had better check them when I get a quiet moment, especially as I haven't looked at them for years I presume they are still in Pandy' she thought.

It was good to see her mum and the family again, who had all come around on the Sunday, mainly to see their mum and it made Georgina's day when her sister Mary told her that Matt Thackery's engagement was off. She was delighted.

When everyone had gone home and, while she was unpacking and getting ready for work the next day, she found Pandy in the cupboard, she snipped the stitches apart under his arm. She had to put her finger in to feel for the stones and managed to drag them out. They were just as beautiful as she had remembered them, sparkling in the artificial light – the colours and size were amazing. She heard her mum moving about so she pushed them back inside Pandy and put him back in the cupboard.

Georgina put plenty of bubble bath in the tub and laid back for a good soak. She had so much to think about. She wondered whether she should go to London to live mainly to improve herself, go to night school and get a better job.

If she was there the ugly man would not be able to find her, she now knew that those stones must be worth a lot of money, but if she went to the police, would they believe her story as to why she hadn't gone to them before. Just because her mum and dad forbade her to go into the wood – was that a good enough excuse, she wondered?

On the other hand, did she now stand a chance of Matt really wanting her – she desperately wanted him. No, she thought, he had upset her so much that she should go and try to forget him, so she would save her money and go to London, that would get her away from all her problems as she felt sure the ugly man would pursue her relentlessly when he needed the money.

Although it would not stop the ugly man from just turning up in Dawlish whenever he wanted. She would need and want to come home every so often so he might still appear out of the blue and get really nasty towards her to get his stones. She must do something with them!

CHAPTER SIX

The ugly man walked up the road, he sat on the old branch of the big fir tree for a while, he could hear music but at first he couldn't make out where it was coming from. He stood on the thick old part of the tree and realised there was a garden over the wall. He thought it looked good and decided to see if there was anything in season he could eat raw. He tried to peer into the greenhouse and then saw a very old man pottering about, it was also where the music was coming from – it sounded like the Home Service.

The escapee thought he would come back that night and hoped the old man would have gone home.

He made his way back to the old orchard, he felt safe there. It wasn't overlooked, the only sign of anyone going in there was where he himself had made pathways through the long grass. It was not raining now, but it was still very cold. He felt miserable and wretched, he was tired, cold and thoughts of Christmas, which was not far off made him feel worse.

He had started a cold, his nose was running and he had developed a chesty cough. He seemed to be continually wet and cold. He was using his dirty prison shirt that now smelled of chicken to blow his nose and he was feeling completely unkempt. He hadn't had a wash for several days.

'I need proper shelter soon. If I managed to get on a train, I would soon be picked up especially as I look so dirty and they probably will never give up looking for me' he thought.

It was dark at about 4.30pm, but there were still people walking and cycling up and down Elm Grove Road, so he thought he would leave a bit later. He looked through his small selection of tools and decided to take all of them including his small Dartmoor prison knife. Leaving the brown leather case full of clothes under one of the corrugated iron sheets, he made his way to the road.

He stood again on the thick branch and peered over the wall. He could see a line of red tile roofing and a roof of corrugated iron. He decided to walk around the wall. There was a wooden seven foot high gate not far from the tree, but he couldn't see over or through it. There was also no visible signs of being able to climb it. He walked to the corner of the wall, even though there was a bank which was full of plants and small bushes, he still could not see over the red brick wall.

The wall turned ninety degrees at the bottom of another garden which, he presumed, belonged to the large house at the top of the road. He couldn't get in there easily and when looking through the hedge, could see that he would be seen from the windows of that house. The wall was hidden by a line of small bushes that were planted about six feet away from it and continued right over to another lane.

He turned and went back to the road. The front of the garden had a ten foot high stone wall with a pair of wooden double doors that would open up to a good eight foot width. The wall then came to a stop and continued at right angles with a thick, well-constructed, six foot wooden fence on top of a three foot high dry stone wall. There was an old fig tree in the corner, which was rambling all over the top of the wooden fence and the stone wall. The fence stretched to the corner of the red brick wall up the narrow lane.

"It's harder to break in here than getting out of Dartmoor prison" he quietly said to himself.

He walked up the very dark Black Cat Lane, he looked at the corner where the red brick wall met the wooden fence. There was some ivy growing up to a height of about four foot. The man scrambled over the fence using the ivy as footholds. He jumped down on the other side and made his way to the greenhouse. What he saw opposite the large greenhouse surprised him. One of the sheds had a light on and smoke was coming out of a small chimney.

'The old man must live here' he thought.

He stood back from the shed and looked in the window. The curtains, if there were any, were not drawn to and there was the old man, sitting by a small range, his head back, his mouth open and snoring quite loudly. Prisoner 1852 was grinning and thinking that he had gone to heaven. This would suit him fine, he could lay low here forever and a day.

He crept to the wooden door of the shed, which was closed with a latch on the door. The prisoner was used to this type of latch and knew exactly how to open the door without making a sound. He was in. The old man, being deaf, never heard a thing, he also never moved a muscle not even when his throat was being cut. The murder was done quickly, quietly and precise. The old prison shirt came in handy again, this time to wipe the blood away from the handle and blade of the knife. The body slumped to the floor.

The prisoner smiled with self-satisfaction. He knew a long time ago, even before being sentenced to spend his days in Dartmoor prison, how to kill.

The body of the old man would normally have felt quite light, but the prisoner was very weak with hunger and exhaustion. He managed to drag his victim to the top of the garden and laid his body on the potato patch.

Feeling no remorse, he returned to the shed and found a stew simmering on the small range. He found several small bottles of beer on the top of the cupboard by the door. He ate and drank the old man's supper without a second thought. Looking around it was an ideal little hiding place. The bed down the far wall was small but long enough even for him. There was the small armchair, a small table and dining room chair by the window and the cupboard on the wall. The small, old black range had a kettle on the top which was just beginning to whistle. The battery wireless on the table was blaring out the 6 o'clock news. The best thing was that it was warm, he knew that another night in the cold wet night air could do serious damage to his health.

He took the kettle and the remains of the stew in the saucepan off the top of the old range then made his way to the small wooden side gate, which he unbolted, then he closed it behind him quietly and made his way to the orchard to pick up the valise. He saw no-one and made his way back to the secret garden.

It was warm and cosy in the little shed, he drew the curtains then, after re-warming the last of the stew and devouring it hungrily, he took another bottle of beer out of the cupboard. He then bolted the door and turned out the paraffin lamp. He eagerly got into the bed without a thought for the poor innocent man lying at the bottom of the garden.

CHAPTER SEVEN

It took all winter to save money for Georgina's pending adventure to move to London, but she knew it would take a lot more to pay for the fare, keep herself for a couple of weeks before she got a job, then she would have to pay bus fares, no doubt, for the first week until pay day. There was a lot to think about and she didn't really want to go to London in her old-fashioned clothes – she needed a lot more money.

It was February when she saw Matt again, she had stayed in over the winter months to save money. Although she felt very hurt by his previous actions she would always forgive him. He was forever in her thoughts.

It was Shirley's birthday and Georgina thought that she couldn't miss out on that celebration. Shirley was a very pretty girl, she had always been such a good friend so Georgina would never miss her pal's birthday bash. Shirley was always a down to earth girl, always smiling, would help any of her friends if needed, and was very popular. Georgina and Shirley often used to share their secrets with one another – knowing that they would never, ever, be retold.

The girls had arranged to meet at the Exeter Inn, after that the plan would be to go into the Royal Hotel where there was a live group playing.

Georgina spotted Matt in the pub and immediately began to wonder how to react if he approached her. She felt quite anxious when she saw him, he hadn't changed and she felt that she loved him so much. She had led herself to believe that he was the best thing that could ever happen to her – he was the nicest man she would ever love. She thought it best to tell him a few little fibs about her absence from weekend life in Dawlish if he asked. It didn't take long, within five minutes he came over to her and asked if she wanted a drink, she saw him coming and smiled – she then made a big fuss of him which he loved. He was fully relaxed and stayed with her all evening.

"Where have you been all winter"? He said.

She was surprised that he even noticed and casually replied "Oh, just spending a lot of time with friends in Torquay".

"I suppose you have been clubbing there too?"

"Sometimes, but mostly going to the pubs then staying the night at my friend Carol's house".

"Carol who?" he mumbled.

"You probably don't know her, I went to the Catholic school with her – we have been friends for years" she lied.

They left the pub and went into the Royal Hotel where a group from Exeter were playing. The place was packed, Matt and Georgina stayed at the bar, she was still only 17 but no-one seemed to bother, so they drank and danced all night. Georgina was the happiest she had been for ages. All the locals were there which was nice for Georgina to see friends that she hadn't seen for a couple of months. The group from Exeter were very good and got a lot of people dancing – it was an excellent night. Georgina hoped it would go on forever.

At about 10.30pm Matt said "Come on, I will walk you home".

Matt took her hand as they strolled across the road to the beach. The cold fresh air really hit them both, because she had had a lot to drink it made her head feel very light but Matt was far worse. They walked under the viaduct, Matt stumbling more than walking, then they turned left and managed to sit on the sand by the bend in the wall and got out of the wind. She soon realised that to try to talk to him about his engagement was out of the question, he was much too drunk for that.

She had been told during the winter, when she stayed in to save money that he had been drinking a lot so it didn't come as a complete shock, but she felt that she was with a person she didn't know. His speech was slurred and he had a very selfish attitude to everything she said. He was quite brutal in his manner and obviously wanted to go much further in sexual relations than Georgina wanted to. Not that he probably could have done anything but he thought he was going to try.

Georgina stood up and said "Come on, I am freezing, I want to go home".

He was angry at what she said and threw her half a crown and told her to get a taxi home. Georgina was so hurt by this, but it did prove that she was right – he was only after sex and when he couldn't get it he reacted really badly. As it was a moonlit night she saw where the coin had landed in the sand, she picked it up and threw it back at him, hitting him on the side of his head.

"I don't want your money" she cried.

Without thinking she then left the beach to walk home – the romantic moonlit night had gone, by the time she had walked to the top of Iddesleigh Terrace the night had turned dark and spooky and she didn't like it at all. She walked along the Exeter Road, which wasn't very busy, too early for the revellers going home to Exeter from the Royal Hotel even though it had just turned 11 o'clock. She managed to give the old water fountain a wide berth, as it was big enough for three girls to sit inside when they were young, she wondered whether someone could hide in there and jump out on an unsuspecting walker.

Her mind was all over the place, she was so upset about Matt's behaviour, she was really worried about the ugly man and frightened of the impending journey up the long Elm Grove Road. Her heart was pounding with fright.

She got to the Catholic Church, which looked really eerie just looming out of the darkness. During the daylight the church was a sandstone colour with a spire made of copper but had, over time, weathered to a green hue. Now the building appeared dark grey against the blackened sky – her imagination was running riot – all she could see was the face of the ugly man wherever she looked.

'Now for the worst bit' she thought, already her heart was thumping loudly, she was sweating even though it was a cold frosty February night. The contrast between the main Exeter Road and Elm Grove Road was so different. Elm Grove Road was a wide country road. She started crying, it was really dark – no street lights until Newlands she reminded herself. If she got to the conker trees she could run, like the wind, past them and then straight past the bottom of Black Cat Lane.

She started running in the middle of the road a long time before the conker trees, her legs seemed to take over, she ran so fast past the school it was as if she was flying. She ran past Mr Birch's market garden, then past Mr and Mrs Shorland's cottage, then the old orchard on the left.

'Oh goodness can I make it all the way home?' She heard herself say.

Frightened by a rustle and movement in the field before the trees made her go faster – she knew it was cows but it didn't make her feel any better. There was a slight bend in the road under the conker trees and when she got there it was like running into a black hole, then she saw shadows as she was coming out of it. Her tears were now stinging her eyes because of her mascara and the coldness of the air which she tried to blink away, but it was like running blind.

The entrance to Oak Park Road, with the post box in the wall was where the ugly man flashed her. Her mind went back to that face, the unkempt, unshaven chin, large nose and small mealy mouth, his hair was messy and seemed to be lank and greasy – his large, partly bloodshot eyes were the worst. She knew she shouldn't have been thinking of him but couldn't get him out of her mind.

The big old fir tree at the bottom of the private road had a branch shaped like a huge saddle on a horse coming out of the old trunk, Georgina thought she saw, out of the corner of her eye, someone sat on the branch, but she didn't stay around to find out.

At the bottom of Black Cat Lane there was a cottage opposite, while running, her eyes were going from left to right quickly not knowing which way to look first. Georgina preferred to glance at the gated entrance to the wood rather than the lane. With the overgrown grounds and drive of Newlands House on the left and the wood on the right she really was scared, even more so when an owl in the wood made his presence known very loudly. She eventually made it to the street light at the bottom of the council estate, several lights were still on in the houses, which made her feel safer.

She was in a terrible state when she eventually slowed down, her black mascara was running down her face, she was sweating profusely, crying like a baby and trying to get her breath at the same time. She really hoped her mother would be asleep when she got home. She cried all the way to the door and kept wondering what had got into Matt, was it the fact that his engagement had turned sour – was his ego bruised that much?

She made a hot drink when she got home, she was now very cold and miserable. Taking the drink and a hot water bottle to bed with her, she lay in the bed and started to cry again, she knew she would, but she had to stifle her sobs - she didn't want her mother to hear. Georgina didn't sleep at all that night. Was she being completely naïve?

All this made her realise that she had to get away. She was so young and wanted better things in life.

CHAPTER EIGHT

The Tuesday after Easter, Georgina boarded the coach to Victoria Station, London. Her mum and Shirley walked with her to the coach station at the playing fields. Her suitcase was not heavy, she hadn't packed much as she had left most of her clothes behind because they were too old-fashioned, but bought her favourite pair of white jeans and a couple of tops, her good pair of court shoes and a couple pairs of sandals. She had set aside £30 to buy new clothes for her job. She also had her best dress and jacket which she was wearing.

She was so excited she couldn't get upset when she kissed her mum cheerio and hugged Shirley, telling them both she would be back for a weekend soon. She was the only passenger getting on at Dawlish so it didn't take long for the coach to be turning out onto the main road.

The journey was long and boring. She ate her sandwiches hungrily and gasped at the sight of Stonehenge. She had seen it from the road many times but always found it compulsive viewing, it fascinated her. She perked up a little when they got to the edge of London. There were so many shops and the coach passed all of the usual attractions.

Uncle Fred and Aunt Lucy met her at Victoria Station and took her to their home. Her room was small and neat with a single bed, wardrobe, chair and dressing table. She had too much room for her few clothes. She slept very well through the night, the street where her relatives lived was a quiet side street, only the locals used it at night. Plenty of people walked down that road to their jobs mainly at Morgan's Crucible factory during the morning and evening.

The next day Aunt Lucy took her to a Recruitment Agency at Clapham Junction. The girls there were very sweet and tried to make Georgina feel less anxious. Sally, a Recruitment Officer was asking her questions from quite a thick bundle of forms that needed to be answered.

"A Levels"?

"No"

"O Levels?"

"No"

"Shorthand?"

"No"

"Typing?"

"No"

"Languages?"

"No"

"Driving?"

"No"

'Oh dear' thought Georgina "they must think I am really thick'.

The girls tested her mental arithmetic and Georgina passed with flying colours, she then felt a lot better.

"Would you like me to contact London University? They need a clerk there and your maths seem reasonable" said Sally, the Recruitment Officer.

"Yes, please" answered Georgina in a very quiet, squeaky voice. She felt really apprehensive because she was out of her comfort zone, but kept thinking she must get over the nervousness otherwise it could hold her back!

Unfortunately, there was only a skeleton staff and no personnel officer working for the next two weeks because it was the Easter holidays at the university. So Sally decided to try elsewhere and continued to look through the card index box.

"Now here's a good job, a clerk needed at Putney, how do you fancy working in the computer industry, would you like me to try for you?"

"Yes, please" Georgina replied.

Although she knew absolutely nothing about computers, what they were about or did, Georgina decided that she must appear to be keen and not crawl back into her shell every time she came across something she had no knowledge of – which was most modern things! After all, Dawlish had never had a roundabout or traffic lights - that was modern technology to Georgina!

Sally managed to get her an interview for that afternoon and informed Georgina that the post was full time, Monday to Friday, 9am to 5pm and the wages were £8-0-0d per week. Sally wrote the address and all the relevant information down on a card.

"Good luck for the interview, I am sure you will settle in well. I came from a small village outside Glasgow, that was nearly a year ago and I love it now, it has changed my life, so I understand how you feel" said Sally".

"Thank you for your help" Georgina replied with a smile.

"Well done" said Aunt Lucy as they walked down the stairs and out onto the street.

"This deserves lunch, it should take less than half an hour to get there".

The building at Upper Richmond Road was a large modern block. They went into the reception area where the concierge checked the list of visitors for the day.

"Oh, yes Miss, you need the third floor Room 16".

Both Georgina and her aunt said "Thank you".

Aunt Lucy sat on the black leather seats in the reception area and the concierge called the lift for Georgina. 'This is the first time I have been in a lift' thought Georgina. The concierge beckoned for her to get in, then pressed button 3.

"Turn right when you get out and go to Room 16".

"Thank you" she replied.

Georgina watched the figures above the doors, then it pinged, 'Time to get out' she thought. 'Turn right, then Room 16' – here we go!

"Come in" called a soft feminine voice just as she knocked gently on the door to Room 16. "Hello, you must be Georgina, please take a seat – Mr Taylor will be here in a moment. My name is Dee, I am Mr Taylor's secretary".

"Thank you" said Georgina once again.

She took particular notice of the secretary, she was about 40 years old, pleasant to look at, her hair, make-up and nails were perfect. She wore a navy blue skirt, which just skimmed her knees, with a white long sleeved blouse that had a Peter Pan collar and her stilettos were navy with a small white bow over her toes. She looked very smart and well groomed.

Dee started to type at a speed that seemed like 100 words per minute and Georgina thought that this is exactly what she wanted – this was her aim.

Mr Taylor appeared in the inter-connecting doorway. He had greying hair and looked about 60-65ish, he had a very kind face and Georgina liked him even before he started to speak.

"Please come in Georgina".

The interview only lasted about 20 minutes, he made her feel very much at ease, and then he offered her the job. Georgina was grinning from ear to ear. He took her to the last room on the right where there was a woman about 30 years old, she had a good figure and a large bust and her hair was put up in a French roll.

The other girl in the room was about the same age as Georgina, she seemed very pleasant but very shy, she also gave the impression that she was from a good family and quite bright.

Mr Taylor introduced them as Yvonne and Anne, they chatted for about 15 minutes then it was time to leave. Georgina was absolutely jubilant by the time the lift had reached the ground floor. Aunt Lucy was so pleased and on the bus home asked her if she would like to play darts that evening for her ladies darts team.

Georgina replied "This day is getting better and better and £8-0-0d a week, that's a fortune. That is nearly four times as much as I was earning in Dawlish".

Before they went home they visited Granny. Georgina loved her gran, she hadn't seen an awful lot of her when Georgina lived in Devon because of the distance, but now she would be able to make up for that. Granny was always a jolly woman, always happy, always laughing and was well known for her generosity (although she never had any money) but she was always able to find a few pennies for her grandchildren. Granny was delighted to see Georgina and was really pleased that she had secured a job and had come to London to live.

On the Saturday, cousin Janet took Georgina shopping to Clapham Junction for some office clothes. She was able to get two cotton dresses, two skirts and blouses, and a cardigan. The clothes were all modern with the right length skirt for business days.

She had never before been so looking forward to going to work.

CHAPTER NINE

Georgina rose early, she looked out of the window at the grey sky and line of red brick houses opposite – she wasn't used to views like that, but it didn't dampen her spirits to get up and make her way to the bus stop. Aunt Lou had already left for work and had given Georgina written instructions on how to get to Upper Richmond Road in Putney.

The children were back at school after the Easter holidays which made the traffic very busy and the buses were a nightmare. The bus stop was crowded, nobody was really queuing as such, not like Dawlish – all orderly. A bus arrived within a few minutes, Georgina looked at her list – she had about four buses to choose from all going to Clapham Junction. The skirmish to get on the bus was eye opening, it was like the survival of the fittest! But she made it. At Clapham Junction she had to cross roads, change buses and cope with traffic lights, all this was new to Georgina – there were no traffic lights in Dawlish. Luckily on the second bus there were not so many school kids and most of them decided to go upstairs making the second half of the journey a lot easier and quieter. She arrived outside the office block with 20 minutes to spare.

"Good morning, Georgina," it was Yvonne.

She had made it to the lift that Georgina was sharing with two others.

Yvonne added "Are you OK, did you have a nice weekend?"

Yvonne showed Georgina where the coffee room was and introduced her to the tea lady, then she picked up an extra cup for Anne. By the time they had got back to the office Anne had arrived. Georgina was shown her desk and the three of them sat and chatted for a while. Yvonne explained a lot of the systems and how this little team worked, its aim and the fire instructions. She added that next Monday Georgina was booked to go on an Induction Course at Head Office.

All-in-all Georgina enjoyed her first day. Everything was different, but most importantly, she felt she could manage the work well.

The Tuesday night was darts night, Aunt Lou and Georgina walked to the pub and met the other members of the team who were really nice. The youngest, Marilyn, was the daughter of Edie, she had volunteered to play darts as well which was good as she was the same age as Georgina. They got on right from the start, Georgina made a name for herself by winning the match point by getting a double two. The ladies exploded with joy. Aunt Lou and the other older ladies were very merry and everyone had a good night.

The following Monday Georgina had to go to Head Office at Putney Bridge. There were about ten others mainly men who were either computer programmers or computer operators. A couple of younger women like Georgina were there, they were also in administration.

The day was interesting, she was informed of the history of the company, its policy, personnel directives, who the American counterpart was etc. After a super buffet lunch they walked, with a member of the Personnel Department, over to Bridge House South where they were shown the computer room.

It was a massive room, at least half again of the Dawlish school assembly room, and it housed a curious machine working a double disc going round in a clockwise direction. The computer operatives wore white coats and hair nets. They were informed that there must never be any dust allowed in that room. They took absolutely no notice of any of those watching from the viewing gallery behind the glass windows. Georgina had no idea whatsoever about these computers and she was too afraid of looking an idiot to ask.

The rest of the week was very pleasant, her position was a busy one and getting to know her colleagues and the work she was responsible for made the days go very fast, she also found that her work was a lot easier than she thought it would be.

Georgina was so pleased that her life was so full and active. Marilyn and her boyfriend Richard took her to Battersea Town Hall where an American Air Force Band were playing the sounds of Glen Miller. What a fabulous night. Georgina went home tapping her toes and thinking this move to London was the best decision she had ever taken. There was always something going on.

During the next couple of weeks, her Gran took a turn for the worse and was admitted to an old folk's home near Wimbledon tennis courts. As it happened, Anne's father was the manager there, so the family knew she would be well looked after, which she was, and once she recovered from the bout of pneumonia Anne used to tell Georgina what kind of week Gran was having when she got to work.

Anne and Georgina arranged that they would go to keep-fit classes on a Thursday, so she visited Gran straight from work, then met up with Anne for an hour's rigorous exercise at Wimbledon. The class was for ladies only and a lot of them needed to go including Georgina, who had put on a lot of weight over the last couple of months.

On the Friday lunchtime, Mr Taylor took the three girls and Dee, his secretary, to a Chinese restaurant in Putney High Street. This was all new to Georgina, she had never seen a Chinese person let alone eat Chinese food – she found it delicious. Mr Taylor announced that he was retiring at the end of the month, he bought a couple of bottles of wine, of which Georgina had never tasted before. The party all seemed a little sad that he was leaving, but pleased for him – he deserved a long and happy retirement.

The weekend came and cousin Janet suggested that they go to see Chelsea v Leeds football match at Stamford Bridge. It was a wonderful atmosphere and the final score was 2-2 draw. Stamford Bridge was packed with young fans, who were all well behaved.

In the evening, Marilyn and Richard had asked Georgina if she would like to go tenpin bowling, he had a cousin coming to stay who was the same age group. Georgina decided to wear her white jeans and took time to put on her make-up. Pete was a really nice chap and they got on very well. It had seemed ages since she had gone on a date and she thoroughly enjoyed it. His clothes were very trendy and he was such good fun. He had come to stay in London to say cheerio to his extended family because he was immigrating to Australia on the £10 scheme. They all had a good evening, which in Georgina's mind went too quickly. After bowling they went to Marilyn's house for coffee then they took Georgina home.

It was the first time since living in London that she had even thought of Matt, this Pete was very much like him apart from that sexy deep voice. Luckily they didn't have too much time on their own to let things get out of hand. He even seemed to kiss like Matt and it made Georgina think about him. How was he? Is he still drinking a lot? Hope he hasn't got a new girlfriend!

She thought about Matt all day on Sunday and even started to feel guilty about not thinking about him before. She decided not to let guilt get to her so she jumped on a bus and went to Paddington rail station and booked a return ticket for the Whitsun Bank Holiday at the end of the month – which was also her mum's birthday weekend.

On the bus home she thought she must look into her finances. She was spending a lot of money because her lifestyle was so busy. She was always out, playing darts, keep fit, shorthand and typing courses and that was just week nights.

On the following Monday morning, someone from Head Office came around to say that they were organising a retirement party for Mr Taylor on the

Saturday evening and everyone was invited.

The party had been organised as a rooftop rendezvous at the top of the Head Office building, 17 floors up, at Putney Bridge. Anne and Georgina were amazed, the views of the river and the park on the Fulham side were wonderful, the decorations, food and drink were all first class. It was a lovely evening albeit quite sad. There were a lot of presumably single chaps there and two of them came over to speak to the girls. Georgina sussed out right away that they were very intelligent young men and spoke well about practically everything, some of which was way out of Georgina's comfort zone. Georgina tried, on several occasions to turn the conversation around to country life and living by the sea, and although they were very polite, it was obvious they knew nothing about nature and just kept the conversation going by talking about the computers which became very boring to Georgina.

She looked at the sky, the moon was bright, and she said to herself 'Well, here I am, I have been enjoying myself so much that I haven't done much about bettering myself intellectually, but I will'.

Another member of staff came around and filled up their glasses. Georgina went home feeling a little drunk but happy.

CHAPTER TEN

As soon as the train rounded the bend at Langstone Rock, Georgina knew she was home, she could smell the sea air. The sun was just setting in the bright red sky, the sea was calm as a mill pond and the beach looked fabulous.

"How could I have left this?" she muttered to herself.

The plan was to meet the girls in the Exeter Inn at about 9o'clock. Georgina managed to get Reg, the local taxi driver, outside the station and asked if he would come back for her in an hour.

Her mum had made a fresh fish and chip supper which was cooking as Georgina had a quick bath. The meal was lovely and she had just enough time to clean her teeth, put on her make-up, do her hair and dress herself.

Mum said "Just go and have a good time with your friends, we have plenty of time over the weekend to catch up on all the news".

"Thanks Mum, I will". Georgina wasn't really listening to her, she was more interested in getting to the pub and seeing Matt.

Just as she was putting on her sandals, her mum shouted, "Just heard your taxi tooting".

"Thanks mum, see you later" Georgina said excitedly.

She gave her mum a quick kiss on the forehead then rushed out.

Georgina arrived at the pub a little late, it was good to meet up with her old friends again, the chatter and laughter from the girls was really loud. The pub was filling up, some of the lads arrived a couple at a time, others on their own.

Georgina thought her heart had stopped when she heard that unmistakeable haunting deep voice.

"Hello maid".

She swung around and there he was.

"You look really well, have you missed me?"

"Of course I have" she replied.

Her legs turned to jelly and everyone in the pub just vanished out of her sight – all she could see was him. It was surreal – it was as if she literally only had eyes for him.

If she had been focusing on other people she would have noticed the strange, ugly man sat in the corner. He didn't approach her at all, but his eyes were on her constantly.

"Would you like a gin and orange?" she heard Matt say above all the noise.

She offered him a cigarette and he lit his lighter, she could feel his wonderful, beautiful, brown eyes staring at her as she bent forward to light her cigarette. When she looked up she noticed his face looked red and tired, she wondered naively, whether he had been sitting in the sun too long.

"I really have missed you darling" he whispered in her ear.

She smiled at him lovingly and then said "What have you been up to since I have been away?"

"Not a lot, been working hard and I am living in a caravan now", he replied.

"Are you?" that is a surprise she thought. She briefly wondered why Shirley hadn't said anything.

"Well, Mum is getting on now and she was finding that I was waking her up when I came home at night at weekends. I don't mean to be, but I am clumsy".

Georgina thought he may also have been very drunk.

"And what about you? He asked. "You seemed to have disappeared overnight, why did you just go off and leave me?"

"The last time you promised to walk me home, I finished up on my own and had to run all the way up Elm Grove Road. You were so drunk, you didn't know what you were doing" she said.

It was unusual for her to speak like that to him but she felt it was needed to be said.

"Sorry, I shouldn't have treated you like that – am I forgiven?"

"You know you are" she said.

He then bent over and kissed her on the cheek then said "Don't worry, I will look after you". He paused then continued "What it will mean is that you will have to stay by my side all night" he said grinning from ear to ear.

"She snuggled towards him and said, "That's fine by me".

The whole evening was theirs until Ernie rang the bell and shouted "Time, Gentlemen Please".

"Do you fancy a coffee at the caravan?" he said.

She nodded and went over to Shirley and the girls who were sat at the long table by the window.

"I'm off now girls, sorry about not chatting too much, can we make up time tomorrow on the beach?"

She didn't really hear their reply because she noticed the slim figure of a man sat in the corner by himself and realised that it was the ugly man. She nearly went into panic mode, she didn't realise that he would still be around. It was then that she noticed his snake and anchor tattoo on his right arm which confirmed that it was the same man.

She grabbed hold of Matt and nearly pushed him out the door.

Matt took her hand and walked to the car, Georgina was trying to hurry him up. It seemed forever for Matt to find the car key in his pocket, find the lock then actually manage to put the key in the door. When they both got in the car Matt wanted a cuddle and Georgina, although frightened was lost in his arms – she knew she wanted to make love to him. The time was right and all thoughts of unwanted babies had disappeared but Georgina was getting anxious she could not see if the ugly man had followed them out of the pub.

'Maybe he already knows where Matt lives' Georgina thought. She was getting really scared.

Matt took his time to drive to the Warren camp site, mainly because he was so drunk. The cold air had hit him for six. Georgina kept looking behind to see if a car was following them. She thought she would ask Matt tomorrow, he was too drunk to ask him tonight if he knows him, or she could ask Ernie, the Landlord of the Exeter Inn – he would know.

He eventually pulled up outside the caravan, which looked quite a modern model from the outside but when she got inside, the carpet squelched when she walked over, it stank of booze and it was very untidy.

'Goodness, bet his mum hasn't seen this, what is going on?' she thought.

He led her to the sitting room area, he went to the fridge and brought out a bottle of gin and a bottle of orange, he leaned over her to get a couple of tumblers that were left on the side.

"How long have you been drinking gin?" she asked.

"Only since I heard you were coming home" he jokingly replied.

He sat beside her after shifting a load of clothes that were thrown on the settee. He had filled three quarters of the tumblers with gin, then just topped it off with orange squash. It was really much too strong for Georgina, so much so that it seemed to burn the back of her mouth. It didn't seem to affect Matt at all. He drank it down easily.

He grabbed her hand and, stumbling, led her into a small dingy double bedroom. Taking the glass out of her hand and putting it on the cupboard, he kissed her with absolute passion and started to undress her. The zip on the back of her pale blue dress came down easily, she let it fall around her ankles, without speaking he then sat her down on the bed and took off her sandals. He carried on kissing her while trying to take off his shirt and trousers. Georgina started to help him but couldn't help feeling that he was kissing and leaning on her to stop himself falling over.

Georgina felt very conscious of her not so good figure so she jumped into the bed and covered herself quickly. He sort of fell in beside her and his warm slightly hairy chest collided with her breasts.

'This is going to be pure passion' she thought.

His hairy legs straddled her thighs at the same time he was kissing her breasts, he seemed to be taking it very slowly and, had not at this time penetrated her. Georgina wanted more, much more.

Suddenly, she heard someone coming in through the front door and squelching their way to the kitchen. Georgina froze.

"Matt, who is that?"

"Just my mate who I share with, don't take any notice of him" he drawled.

The person outside was heavy footed, stumbling about, knocking into things and then started singing in a drunken manner. Georgina felt so vulnerable again.

It took Matt just a couple of minutes to start snoring and Georgina thought she was safer where she was rather then make a dash for it – she was too scared to even try.

'Surely this cannot be the ugly man?' she asked herself.

She lay in the bed thinking it through. It could not be the ugly man because Matt gave no sign of acknowledging him in the pub, he never said hello or goodbye to him.

The noise started to get quieter from the kitchen as he moved down the hallway to a second bedroom, she heard him slump down onto the bed and within seconds snoring came from that direction as well. It was easy to hear through the paper thin walls.

Tears started to roll down her cheeks, she felt so frustrated and upset to think that Matt had gone down this drinking path – he had so much going for him and although she would forgive him anything it was hard to understand why he was letting himself go like this. She never in all her life imagined that this would happen – but why did she still love him so much?

The awful smell of old booze permeated the whole caravan. The curtains were very thin and she could see, between them, the stars twinkling surrounding a crescent moon.

She stared at the view and thought 'Oh, please, please let this all be a dream, let me wake up in my own little bed at my mum's house'.

Matt woke at 9 o'clock, Georgina had not slept at all, she had been too nervous to move until then so she started to get dressed when Matt got up.

"I'm sorry maid, I was useless last night".

"How long have you been drinking like this? She asked.

"DON'T GET AT ME, YOU SOUND JUST LIKE MY MOTHER" he bellowed. His voice sounding really angry and loud.

She noticed that his hands were shaking badly and his attitude had changed dramatically. Georgina couldn't understand this at all. She had seen him drunk before but this was a lot worse.

She followed him into the kitchen to put the kettle on. His mate was breathing heavily in the other bedroom, the noise was partly snoring and, to Georgina, sounded like partly death rattle. She knew where he was so she kept an ear towards that room all the time in case he came out.

The smell of old beer and cider was horrendous, perhaps opening a window might help, she thought, but before she could do that she opened the fridge to get the milk – and quickly closed it again. It stank and traces of mould were everywhere. She had seen enough.

"Please take me home Matt" she pleaded.

CHAPTER ELEVEN

The prisoner slept soundly and didn't wake until 10 o'clock. He came to and momentarily didn't know where he was. Then it all came back to him. He snuggled back into the bed and imagined that he had 'inherited' a secret garden and was keen to explore but he found the bed and the room so comfortable and warm he thought he would lie in for a while.

After putting some small branches on the fire, and watching it spark up with an old newspaper, he made a cup of coffee and decided the first job would have to be removing all the ivy growing up the fence, he felt that if he could get in so could someone else. He shivered as he went outside of the shed. He noticed the inside of the double doors in the stone wall, by the road, were bolted top, bottom and middle.

'Good idea to have your doors bolted, never know if a murderous butcher is roaming about these days' he sniggered to himself.

His eyes went to the well just to the left of the gates, he strode over to it, cupped his hands together, looked at the water then smelt it. It seemed fine so he took a small sip and decided it was fresh and clear. The corrugated rooved shed in the corner, on the other side of the big fir tree, also had double doors. When he opened them he found an old Ford car, the key was still in the ignition, he got in and turned the key, it fired first time. He stood on the running boards and checked the trafficators – they both worked and so did the lights inside them, he then tried the side and headlights. After checking all four tyres, he decided that everything was in a road worthy condition. He didn't want the police to flag him down if he drove it to town. This made him feel very happy.

There were two other sheds next to the one he had just slept in. One had every kind of tool that any gardener would ever need, he grabbed a spade – it was in immaculate condition. Nice and clean and sharp. The next shed had been used as a 'potting on' shed with every size terracotta pot imaginable. He found three sacks, one of potatoes, one of carrots and one of onions and there was also a pile of swedes and parsnips on the workbench.

It had started to rain heavily, he heard a clap of thunder as well, so he went back into Shed No1 and made another cup of coffee. While he was there, sitting in the warm shed, his mind started going back to how his life had taken the rotten path.

The prisoner liked gardening, he learned a lot from the prison gardens. He never had such pleasures when he was growing up in Birmingham. His father had left his mother with four children and the only way she could make a living was by going onto the streets at night. He had no home life, hardly any schooling, he didn't even know where his brothers or sisters were. He was first 'put away' in a children's home that was where he learnt burglary, theft and pickpocketing, when he came out he didn't know where his siblings had gone. After his first spell in prison for burglary he didn't care where his siblings had gone.

His second spell in prison was for murder and this time he went straight to Dartmoor. He had seen a house which he thought would be easy to burgle but didn't take into account that the owner was a formidable woman, who had travelled the world, was very street wise and owned two very large half wild dogs to protect her.

He climbed in through a small open window in the kitchen, he did not know there were dogs in the house for there was no sign of them. He had had so much experience in creeping around that he made no sound at all. The house was in darkness, but his night vision was good and he made his way to a room which he thought would be the Library. He was looking for a safe. There didn't appear to be one, he rifled through the drawers of the desk and found nothing. It was the same in the other downstairs rooms.

As he made his way up the wide staircase he thought he could hear a noise coming from one of the bedrooms. It was a bedroom at the back of the house, he saw a light shining under the door. It was obvious someone was in there listening to a radio broadcast. He managed to slip into a front bedroom, but the room was empty, the same in the second room. The third, he thought, may be a bathroom.

He had come this far, he thought he might just as well carry on into the room where the noise was coming from. He felt confident that he would be able to overcome whoever was inside the room. He turned the door handle silently then gently pushed the door open. Suddenly, and of great shock to him, the two dogs came bounding towards him.

He quickly closed the door behind him and retreated, but before he could get to the staircase, as quick as a flash a woman had opened the door, the dogs came straight for him and, one attacked him from the side, the other was biting his ankles from behind. They had him on the floor in no time.

The woman called the dogs off, they were so obedient they immediately let him go and sat beside her like a pair of statues.

"What do you want" the woman bellowed.

He had no choice but to come clean and he just muttered "money". He was really angry, he hated dogs at the best of times, he never saw them when he had recced the house the week before.

Although she looked quite elderly, she was made of strong stuff and appeared to be quite fit. He thought, while the dogs were beside her, he would make a run for it, but she was too clever for him and as soon as he started to move she signalled the dogs to attack. They both pounced on him and were biting his lower arms and legs which resulted in him collapsing on the floor again.

He was now at the top of the stairs, the screw driver that had been in his pocket was now in his hand, he started lashing out towards the dogs, one was trying to bite his face so he stabbed that one in its chest, the other was still biting his foot and drawing blood, he managed to get the other dog's body off him and he rammed the screwdriver straight into the side of the gnawing dog's neck. He howled then went quiet.

The woman was horrified that anyone could harm her beloved dogs, so she went over to get the man off of the dogs, he stood up, seized her by her upper arms and threw her down the stairs, she landed only a few steps down. Somehow she survived this and in her rage went back up the stairs and kicked him in the groin area. He doubled up in pain and sank to his knees. Then she kicked him down the stairs.

Her strength was beginning to sap, she made her way slowly down to a hall telephone. She managed to stride over his body and phoned the police. It was while she was talking to a police officer that he came from behind her and smashed the screw driver right through her wind pipe. The police could hear this and because she was a Justice of the Peace they knew her and where she lived, which was down the road from the Police Station, they immediately sent a couple of police cars straight to her house.

It took him a while to get his breath and recover from the beating he had received to his testicles. Just as he was leaving the house through the front door, two policemen were waiting for him and he was put in a cell within fifteen minutes. Never before had a woman fought back and injured him so much. His dislike towards women was getting as strong as his hatred of dogs.

When his case went to court, he was sentenced to 30 years imprisonment at Dartmoor prison.

Sitting back in the little hut, his thoughts started to fade and he noticed the weather had cleared a little so he went outside and continued to follow the path around the garden, there seemed to be plenty of the brassicas, there was a rhubarb bed, but they seemed a bit small, but not much else to eat at this time. There were four fruit trees, a south facing wall had raspberry or Loganberry canes tied to the wall with a strawberry bed in the front and there were also a couple of rows, of what looked like, white, red and blackcurrants and a row of gooseberries. He checked the greenhouse and to his delight there were about twelve three foot high canes, probably for tomatoes, winter lettuce and a big grape vine. He was delighted with what he saw, he was also in awe of the old knowledgeable gardener. He stood in different places around the garden and found that he could see no windows or doors or people. He could have been on a desert island.

He started to dig a grave, it took him several hours of hard work. Before he buried the old gardener he went through the old man's pockets and found a small roll of gardener's string, a very sharp Swiss army knife, an old pipe and some tobacco, a lighter and a beautiful old silver pocket watch. He put all of his finds into his pockets.

He then dragged the body closer to the grave. He was in such awe of the old man's gardening expertise that he went back into Shed 1, grabbed the Warder's coat, which was heavy through being so wet and then wrapped it around the body. Letting the body fall into the grave, he then mumbled a few words of the only prayer that he knew. He was very careful about covering his tracks, so he made sure he shovelled all of the blood stained earth into the grave on top of the body. He then filled it in and made it look as if he had just dug up some potatoes.

He fetched all of his prison clothes, he thought he would keep the trousers and wash them – he now has soap and water so he could smarten them up. He burnt his other clothes and the warder's hat on the old bonfire patch.

He thought 'That's my old life gone now I am going to start a better one'.

He stood and watched until it was just a pile of ash. The chicken grease on the shirt helped it to burn. While in that corner by the fig tree he found a little old shed with a self-composting toilet by the front stone wall and a well turned compost heap by that same east facing wall.

He then took a chance and went outside through the small wooden gate and made his way around to Black Cat Lane and stopped by the corner with the red brick wall. He could easily see the ivy growing up the wall and fence and, because he was tall he could stretch and snip it at the bottom, he ripped it from the uprights easily and, luckily, it had not left any growth marks.

"Good job done, now I am truly safe" he remarked to himself.

It started to rain again, so he went into shed No 1, the old range was burning brightly so he put the kettle on again. The old man certainly had it all worked out. There was a really huge line of logs up against the wall in the shed where the car was kept, he went through the cupboards and found plenty of tins of meat, corned beef, spam, packets of tea, biscuits, baked beans, Camp coffee, a couple of ounces of tobacco and twelve bottles of beer. He thought he could live like a King forever. He wondered why his luck had changed so much since he came to Devon. He loved Devon, He had never in all his life been so rich and comfortable.

He also saw a small chest of drawers beside the bed. There were socks, vests, pants, jumpers and trousers. Underneath the old coats on the back of the door there was a decent coat and raincoat which fitted him well, albeit a little short.

What pleased him more than anything was an old biscuit tin he found in the bottom drawer beside the bed. He opened it with no great expectations, but to his delight he found the old man's hand written Last Will and Testament, duly signed by a priest and dated about 20 years previous. There was no mention of a solicitor, which pleased him, he was leaving it all to a dog's home, somewhere in Somerset.

"They're not having it - I hate dogs" he said to himself.

He looked through the tin and found a picture of, presumably, the old gardener and his wife on their wedding day, her birth and death certificate, his birth certificate and their marriage lines, there was also a picture of a baby, a birth certificate for a Master Anthony Davis, also a death certificate for a Master Anthony Davis aged 6 months. The birth certificate was registered in Wales, but the death certificate was registered in London.

"Well, well, he thought. Just a year younger than me. Ideal, I will become the new Anthony Davis, date of birth 12 October 1932, preferably known as Robert" he chuckled. He threw the baby's Death Certificate in the fire.

In amongst the certificates, there was the car's Registration Document, but no insurance. He pondered about this – maybe the old boy didn't drive? He put the Registration Document with the birth certificate back in the tin. There were various other letters and receipts, of which he read all of them. Thinking that there was nothing of great importance, and it really looked as though there were no heirs or bank accounts he ripped them all up along with the photo and the other certificates and threw them in the range.

The most exciting find was the Deeds to the one acre plot of land and about £100 in cash. That was an extraordinary amount of cash to be left in a tin. He really couldn't believe his luck.

"It's mine now, all mine. If anyone asks in the future, I will just say the old man sold it to me and I haven't seen him since" he said with utter glee.

On the table, by the Roberts radio there was a wooden box with brown paper bags partly full of self-gathered seed, all marked with the names of the flowers and vegetables and the dates collected. He could not have wished for anywhere better to hide away. He thought he was set for life.

CHAPTER TWELVE

When Georgina went back to work, after her break in Dawlish, her first surprise was that, when she received her pay cheque, she had accrued £10 in overtime and had received a £2 birthday rise per week. She felt she needed a little bit of good news because she was feeling very low about how Matt had treated her and also - was his lodger the ugly man? Every couple of minutes she thought about that. Was he following her? Did he know she had the stones? Surely not after all this time - she wasn't sure about anything anymore, but what she was sure about was that next time she went back to Dawlish she would find out about those damn stones and whether the police would prosecute her for hiding them.

The other bit of news was that her department would be moving to Reading in October and would Georgina like to go with them. Georgina immediately made up her mind that no, she would not like to go to Reading. She explained this to her boss there and then and he assured her that they would find her a new position at Putney Bridge.

The next night was a darts night, it was local so Aunt Lucy and Georgina left home about 7 o'clock. When she got to the pub she realised that it was the same pub that she had met up again with Simon. She wondered whether it was still his local.

The game started on time and it was a close shave, but Aunt Lucy beat her player which meant they had won the match. Once again it was Georgina who won the straight leg with a double two. The ladies shouted for joy.

Someone at the bar, it was a man's voice shouted "Well done Georgina".

'I know that voice' she thought.

She looked towards the bar and there was Simon, looking as handsome as ever, his blonde hair now quite fashionably long.

"Oh Simon, how lovely to see you again" she said, as she made her way to the bar.

"I have often dreamt of this meeting, but after the last time we parted, I wasn't expecting such a nice welcome".

"I should have thought you knew me better than that".

"You're looking well" he said.

"I've just come back from Dawlish after a week's holiday in the sun".

"Are you living here? He said surprisingly. "Now that your cousin Paul has immigrated to Australia, I never hear any news about you".

"I have been living here for nearly six months, I work at Putney and really like it. What's your news?"

"Well, I am still working as a printer for a newspaper in Fleet Street. I still like it, the money is good, on the downside, I don't like the shift work, I have just finished now at 10 o'clock and next week I am on nights, ugh".

He smiled then added "No doubt you can make me feel better about that".

She grinned. He then pulled her closer to him and kissed her on the cheek. He asked for her telephone number and said he would like to take her out after the week of night work.

The girls in the darts team all cheered after the kiss, they all agreed he was handsome. Aunt Lucy wanted to know where she had met him and as soon as she said he was cousin Paul's friend that was OK. Georgina was so excited about meeting up with him again, he and Matt were the first men that she truly admired.

She walked home with Aunt Lucy and had decided that she was going to be very careful about trusting him, she thought that she must give him a chance.

'But he is so handsome surely he could attract a girl far prettier than me. I must not get too close – he will let me down' she thought.

It was such a whirlwind month, everything seemed to happen at once. Simon phoned and arranged to take her out the following Friday after his turn of nights. Georgina was really pleased about that but still had the old pangs about Matt.

She went back to work and was invited to attend an interview for a position with a Manager called Stuart Barrington. The interview was to be held the next day at Bridge House North in Fulham. Georgina arrived about ten minutes early and reported to the concierge. He looked at his list of visitors then phoned Mr Barrington's secretary, Phyllis.

She arrived and took Georgina to her office, which she shared with another secretary Ivy, they both seemed very pleasant. Mr Barrington was a young quiet handsome Scot. He immediately introduced her to a young chap called Colin who was gathering information to make an encyclopaedia of computer errors and needed a clerk/typist to help. After a short time Georgina was offered the position, she accepted even though she had no speed when typing.

On the Friday night, Simon came to pick her up in his van. They hit it off immediately. She had worn her brown dress with orange flowers on it. They started the evening at the Eight Bells in King's Road, Chelsea, then going to other pubs that he seemed to be known in. He introduced Georgina to his friends and their girlfriends and she was able to join in their conversations which really pleased her. In particular she enjoyed the company of Mo and Maurice, Sally and Mike, Pat and Dawood and Barbara and Trevor. They were all intelligent people and good fun, they made her feel welcome to their little circle and was very helpful when Georgina asked any questions about the London nightlife or fashion.

While Simon was driving her home, Georgina told him that she had had a very nice evening and enjoyed their company. She also mentioned that on the following Sunday she was walking from Windsor to Wandsworth with Anne from work for the Charity 'Homes for the Homeless', it was about 30 miles but all on roads and pavements so it should be easier than Ten Tors. Simon seemed very proud of her and sponsored her for £10.00

He took her home and after spending about ten minutes in the van he asked if he could take her out again.

"I could find out what's on at the pictures" he said.

"OK, I would like that, haven't been to the pictures for ages. Let me know what time, goodnight Simon".

He kissed her for a long time and she enjoyed his closeness. His arm muscles seemed to hug her tightly and she felt very safe and secure.

"Goodnight Georgina, sleep well".

It was now 11 o'clock and Georgina went indoors, she was feeling really tired and needed some rest before Sunday.

Georgina was excited about this date with Simon as she had liked him for years. She wore her maroon coloured, fashionable dress, she always liked the empire line dresses like Dusty Springfield always wore. She managed to team this dress with a pair of white plastic kinky boots. She felt good, her hair was long and flowing – she still could not put on the thick black make-up on her eyes, she felt better without it, no matter how fashionable.

"You look fabulous" said Simon.

Georgina was overjoyed.

When they came out of the cinema, Georgina snuggled into Simon's coat. She said she was cold but really it was because she just wanted to be close to him. They then went into the pub close by and had a drink in there. The pub was packed so it took a while for Simon to find his friends. They found a couple of seats and then his 'friends' came and joined them. They were not the friends that Georgina had met before. These were totally different, these young men seemed to be an aggressive lot, their language was appalling and they were only interested in causing mayhem.

Georgina drank her drink quite quickly and then, to her relief, she heard the landlord shout "Time Gentlemen Please". Simon was lingering, the other young men were also biding their time whilst running down the Tories.

One of the men said "We're going to Chelsea for coffee, fancy coming?"

Simon turned to Georgina and said "Do you fancy coffee?"

"Rather not, if you don't mind Simon, I have to be up really early tomorrow. Perhaps another time, is that alright with you? She said.

When they got home, Simon said "Of course, you're on your walk tomorrow aren't you? I am on 6am to 2pm shift next week, so can we meet up next Friday night, I will phone you to see how you got on?"

"Love to and thank you for a nice evening"

"Good luck for tomorrow" he said as she was getting out of the van.

Sunday arrived and she had to be at Windsor at 8 o'clock in the morning. Anne's Father came to give Georgina a lift. The day was a bit chilly, but that was good, it meant they could warm up on the walk. It seemed reasonably easy compared to Ten Tors. Georgina, Anne and her sister Helen completed the walk in a reasonably good time.

Georgina was so pleased to get home, have a hot bath and rest her poor feet. It didn't take her long to jump into bed and was asleep in no time.

CHAPTER THIRTEEN

Life going out with Simon was very exciting at first, he was thoughtful, kind and good fun. He made her laugh. The down side, which took some time to rear its ugly head, was the fact that he was overly politically minded. It took Georgina some time to realise it. She had no knowledge of politics of any persuasion. She had never been interested in it.

He asked Georgina, one night sitting in the pub, if she would like to go to a Peace Rally. She really was totally naïve and knew nothing, or of anyone in politics, apart from the Prime Minister Harold Wilson. She only knew of him because his son was going to marry a Dawlish maid, her father taught Georgina music when she attended the Secondary Modern School. She also knew his daughter from the Girl Guides.

"Come on, Georgina, please come, it will be a nice day out, we will be protesting about the American's invading Vietnam. We can meet up with friends of mine – it will be great day" he assured her.

She agreed to go.

"We will be better going by bus, can you meet me say at 9.30 next Sunday morning at the end of Park Gate Road? Make sure you wear comfy walking shoes" he said smiling.

"OK" said Georgina in all innocence.

She did briefly wonder whether his horrible friends would be there, but thought that they would be able to lose them, and as she loved to be in Simon's company she didn't want to say no.

Aunt Lucy was not happy about Georgina going to the Rally.

"Oh, Georgina, you must be very careful. Who are these people that you are going to meet? These Rallies can sometimes get completely out of hand.

"I will be OK, Simon will look after me".

Regardless of what Aunt Lucy had told her Georgina decided to go anyway.

She met Simon as arranged and they made their way to Trafalgar Square by bus. As they neared the Square and the surrounding roads they noticed, that instead of a couple of thousand people, there were far more people there than that – more like 25,000 people. There were hundreds of people making their way to the Square from every road.

The Peace Rally was against the American invasion of Vietnam and the atrocities that were reputedly going on there. Even before the Rally started, young men were showing their anger. Simon had arranged to meet his, so called, 'friends' outside a small tobacconist not far from Trafalgar Square. His friends were already there and spitting their venom.

Georgina didn't like any of them. She could see exactly what Aunt Lucy meant within the first thirty minutes of being there. What horrified Georgina most was Simon! He was like a sort of monster, certainly not the Simon that she thought he was.

A series of speeches were underway. Parts of these orations were of passion and of real justification towards the invasion. Other diatribes were just anti everything and the baying mob were trying to justify their reason for being there.

The Rally started quite well. It wasn't until the mob got to the United States of American's Embassy at Grosvenor Square that things really got out of hand.

Shouting, jostling and shouts of 'Ho, Ho, Ho Chi Minh' were getting louder. Some idiots were throwing smoke bombs in amongst the crowd of spectators, the sound of breaking glass could be heard above the whistles, shouts and chants. Then the police on horseback arrived. Those protestors with any sense stood back away from them, others were throwing rocks and other missiles towards the horses. It was very frightening and difficult to get away from, whichever way Georgina looked there was fighting, kicking and spitting.

Georgina had seen enough. She wanted to go home. Momentarily she had seen Simon, his bright yellow shirt visible through the crowd. To her horror, she watched as he attacked a policeman for no reason. Another policeman joined in to try to keep him under control, they held him by his hair and his arms but he was kicking them in absolute fury. When they did free his arms he was punching the younger policeman, blood was flowing from the poor man's nose after he had tripped over another protestor. She was terrified.

She lost sight of him when a surge of people came down a road leading to the Square. They seemed to lift Georgina off her feet, she was trapped by a mass of people. She found it difficult to breathe as she was jammed into the heaving bodies like a sardine as she was carried on the tide of people. The crowd then started to sway uncontrollably.

She could feel herself about to faint, she was hot and the sweat was pouring down from her brow. Most of these feelings were sheer terror.

"Don't fall down. Don't fall down" she could hear herself saying to a young woman on her left.

Her advice, although good, was very difficult to do. She felt that her body was swaying to almost 90 degrees, but her feet were only just on the floor. When it subsided a little, she managed to push and fight her way to the edge of the procession. She was shaking with fear. Not knowing where she was, she thought the best way home would be beside the river. Even if she knew the way, the buses would probably be trapped in the traffic due to the rally. She walked away from the crowd and saw a policewoman across the side road.

"Which way to the river please?" she asked.

The policewoman pointed, luckily, to the way she was heading.

Georgina wanted to have a drink before walking home but the cafes close to Grosvenor Square were all boarded up. There were still a lot of people down on the embankment, she thought it best to get away as soon as possible, there seemed to be a strange atmosphere and she was worried that trouble could flare up anywhere.

Georgina crossed the bridge and continued to walk up-stream eventually getting to Battersea Park. It had taken a long time to get there but she felt so much better. She was hoping that she would not be seen by Simon's mum and dad, who would ask her questions about his whereabouts. Once inside the Park, instead of taking the direct route along the avenue of chestnut trees, she made her way to another road, that would take her a longer way home, rather than risk seeing them by going the shorter way – it took an extra half hour, but she preferred this.

Aunt Lucy was pleased to see her "Oh, Georgina, you are home a lot earlier than I thought you would be – are you and Simon alright?" she said".

Georgina started to cry. "I am so sorry, I should have taken notice of what you said. It was really scary. I lost sight of Simon and walked home on my own".

The hot bath made Georgina feel very tired so she went straight to bed, she didn't want Aunt Lucy to start asking questions about Simon or his friends. She had no answers as to why he was like this. It made Georgina think that it was history repeating itself under a different guise.

'Why do I pick these men? I cannot continue seeing Simon after his performance this afternoon, I don't think I could trust him again. I knew he would let me down.' She thought.

CHAPTER FOURTEEN

Prisoner 1852 was eager to get out of bed. The winter had been long and cold but he had been living well and was fully rested. The radio had kept him company, he had tuned in to the national and the local news at lunchtimes so was kept abreast of all that was happening. There had not been any bulletins about the 'escaped Dartmoor prisoner' for a couple of months, so he felt quite safe. He wasn't so stupid to think they had given up – he just thought that once again he was ahead of them and now that he was established in his 'secret garden' he could relax a little.

His experience working in the prison gardens had stood him in great stead. He knew he should wait until the spring came to see what came up in the garden. He was especially pleased when he found, on the wall of Hut No 3, a plan of crop rotation which made him start to seriously think about the coming season.

He dug over the area where he had buried the body, according to the plan that was where the potatoes had been last year. This year, was going to be where the cabbages would go. He had planted most of the seeds in trays and they were sitting in the semi-warmth of the greenhouse.

He wondered whether in readiness for next winter, he could fix a pipe from the fire in his 'living shed' into the tool shed next door, where he had found, on the other side of the wall, an old brick boiler with a fire underneath. Instead of using that fire he could use half the tool shed to make a bathroom. All he needed was some piping and a tin bath. Or he could run a pipe to the greenhouse across the path to heat the greenhouse, or at least take the chill off of it. There were times, in his 'living' shed that it seemed to be very hot, much too hot for him now that he is fit and well. He started to look in every nook and cranny, all the areas under the rooves to find some piping that would do the job, but he found none. As he had done a basic plumbing course at Dartmoor, he wondered whether he would be able to tackle this job, he would try anyway but would have to buy the pipes.

"That's another job for later" he said to himself.

It took him several days to dig over the large vegetable patch and then another day and a half to dig it over again. The Dawlish soil was good, he could tell this by the number of anemones and violets that had grown in the flower garden. He planted his spring onions at Easter, then his carrots and found lots of bean and pea sticks and put them in place for sowing later. He planted about a quarter of the sack of potatoes, those that had not gone to seed he kept back for eating.

He wasn't a brilliant cook, but he managed to survive on vegetable stews which were tasty and hot. He was lucky. It wasn't long before it would be summer and the salad crop that he had grown from seed, would soon be ready for harvest.

Although the garden kept him busy during the day, it was the evenings that he found boring. The sound on the radio was going quieter, he knew it was the batteries, his log pile needed replenishing and his food cupboard was getting to look like 'Old Mother Hubbard's' which meant he would have to go out.

The thought of life on the outside was exciting and scary. He didn't want to lose the garden that he had 'bought' – he would fight to the death for that, but he needed to have a more varied diet and his log pile needed replenishing before winter.

His thoughts and urges, that he had been having every night and day, about having a woman again was becoming more and more urgent. He knew he had to do something and soon.

One morning he woke up and decided straight away that he would go out. The radio crackled and went dead the evening before and he realised, for the first time, that he was totally alone. The thought was worse than solitary confinement, at least in solitary he would see the guard twice a day. He realised that he hadn't spoken to or seen anyone up close since before he killed the guard on Dartmoor, that was some time ago now, he couldn't remember when exactly.

He put on the longest pair of trousers he had, a nice shirt, it was too hot for anything else. The welly boots he had been wearing belonged to the old gardener, he had cleaned up his prison supply shoes one rainy day when he had nothing to do, so he was ready for his adventure.

He was full of expectation, he was like a kid with a new bike. He had found a key to the small side gate and carefully opening it, he poked his head out and saw no-one. He quickly slammed the door behind him. He was out in the world alone.

It took him only a couple of minutes to get to the main Exeter road. He turned left this time to avoid Dawlish. He could see over the wall that the sea was calm, he could swim and thought one evening he would go down to the beach and have a much needed good wash down.

After about a ten minute slow walk he came to three small shops and a garage. There was a Post Office, a grocery shop and a sweet shop. He tentatively went into the Post Office first and bought a newspaper, then he went into the grocery shop and bought the batteries for the radio, more tea, coffee, tins of everything, tobacco, more beer, soap, biscuits, cheese, bread, bacon and eggs and treated himself to a bottle of milk. The shop assistant put all his shopping into two brown paper carrier bags and thanked him for his custom.

No-one seemed to take any notice of the tall stranger. He had worried a little before going into the shops in case he was recognised, he has a lot to lose now. He made it back to the garden confident that he would be able to go out again even though his heart was racing when walking fast up Elm Grove Road. He was pleased to be back in the garden that was where he felt safe. The string handles on the carrier bags had been cutting into his hands but he didn't care, he was just relieved to be back safe.

The next morning he woke quite late. He had been hoeing in the garden after his shopping trip the day before and it was beginning to get a bit monotonous. He thought a break would do him good so he washed, shaved and made his way through the side gate and out onto the road.

He decided to sit on the old tree branch and test whether there was anyone around, but after only a couple of minutes a pretty little girl came cycling down the road and stopped at the post box. Although he wouldn't normally touch children, he felt randy and really felt he needed a woman.

He wanted to show someone, anyone of the opposite sex, that he was powerful. He wanted to draw attention to himself and in control of any situation especially a sexual one. He decided to flash just to see her reaction. The little girl was nervous, she was a little too young for it to make an impression, she just got on her bike and went back up the road. This reaction was a surprise to him. He began to have depressing thoughts that he was invisible or that his manhood wasn't up to the job. He tried to put these thoughts out of his mind, he knew he had a good physique and manly appearance and carried on walking down the road.

He was feeling sexy and could only think of a voluptuous woman, he thought he would walk along the beach to see some females in their bikinis. He went down to Coastguards beach where there were a lot of women, he sat and watched them for ages but that just made him more wanting. He resisted the temptation to do anything – he would surely get caught here. He started to walk along the beach, trying not to stare for too long at the women there.

As he walked closer to the wooden Black Bridge, he walked over it and found himself in Sea Lawn Terrace. He walked up the hill, turned left at the main road and walked back up Elm Grove Road. He had a thought that he could cut off a pair of the old gardener's trousers to the knees to make a pair of swimming trunks, there was a pair of very sharp garden scissors in Shed No 2. He would go for a swim later one evening when there wouldn't be quite so many people around.

The next day, while looking in the wood for small fallen trees for his fire, he came across a big white painted house and thought there must be some valuables in there – but he had second thoughts.

'I have everything I want, apart from a woman to have sex with, so why put myself in a position to get caught and be back in jail? He asked himself.

He carried on his walk, he wanted a hiding place for the gems that he stole from the house just outside Chudleigh. Thinking seriously about capture the day before, he was keen to hide the stones rather than 'keeping all his eggs in one basket'. He heard a lot of kids, they were playing by the old tin shed at the edge of the wood, he wasn't worried about them, they seemed to be in the field rather than the wood.

About 20 yards past a large pit in the wood he saw, in the distance, a fair sized boulder which tapered to a point. He counted the strides from an old fir tree to the boulder then with his hands he dug a small pit, he dropped the bag of stones into the hole then covered it completely with woodland ground litter.

CHAPTER FIFTEEN

Several years later, the escaped convict decided to go into Dawlish one evening. He was managing to control his feelings for sex with great difficulty.

He was in no hurry, thinking that he would go down to town later, he needed to be careful – he had a lot to lose now. He snoozed in his garden chair in the late evening sunshine after his tea. When he awoke he was feeling really in need of a woman, any woman would do, so he hurried to get out and find a female. He could have picked a house to burgle but really didn't want to take the chance of getting caught. He knew that they would throw the book at him this time and he would probably be given two life sentences for the murder of the Warder at Dartmoor prison and the Justice of the Peace.

He walked along the beach to the viaduct, where he caught sight of a young teenager at the bus stop. It was dark now and the town was quiet, no-one else was around and there was hardly any traffic either.

"She should be easy" he thought.

He walked quietly and casually towards the bus stop and when she turned to look in the direction of the Blenheim Hotel he struck. He held the old gardener's Swiss army knife close to her back and whispered in her ear.

"Walk towards the beach, if you scream or resist in any way I will kill you" he said.

She obeyed because she was so frightened. He was completely out of his mind with anticipation and frustration. The smell of her cheap perfume sent him dizzy with desire and need. He had an erection as soon as his fingers touched the young smooth skin of the girl's neck. Keeping the knife to her throat with one hand, he put his other arm around her chest and felt the pert nipples on her small breasts through her blouse.

Under the viaduct she started to resist by putting her feet firmly on the concreted walkway, she needed to try to find the wall so that she could put her feet on it to act as a brake, but he kept her away from the wall so she couldn't reach it. The waves were rough and making a lot of noise when the full power of the sea crashed against the break wall then the ebb tide dragged the shingle on the outgoing wave. Screaming was lost to the sound so she started to struggle against him but he was so strong he dragged her to the steps behind the beach cafe and threw her down them in rage, she caught her head on the stone wall and landed spread eagled on the small area of sand that had not been touched by the high tide. She lay completely still, blood pouring from her temple on the left side of her head. He didn't know, or care, whether she was unconscious or dead. The latter making him feel more in control, more powerful and needier due to his years of enforced celibacy, it made him desire her more if she were dead. Even had she been alive she wouldn't have stood a chance. With complete disregard to her wellbeing and with no shame or guilt – he cruelly raped the body of the young girl.

The next day when the body was found by a local fisherman, the police roped off the viaduct and Main Beach and a Detective Inspector was sent from London to organise the investigation into the young girl's rape and murder.

Detective Inspector Neil Morris arrived by train in Dawlish at 1300hrs. As he sat on the train deep in thought, he looked wistfully out of the window, he thought that if he was successful on this case he would surely get promotion early. Climbing the professional ladder was the most important thing to him. He was a good looking, physically attractive, middle aged man who thought women were playthings. He treated all women disrespectfully, especially the attractive ones. He used and abused them.

He also thought very little of country people especially those that lived south of Bristol. DI Morris was under the impression that they were all stupid and had no education, compared to people living in cities and large towns.

The Police Forensic Officer had been called as well as the Home Office Pathologist, who was in charge. After a meeting with the DI, the Pathologist gave permission for the body to be taken to the Mortuary after a full search of the area and swabs taken of blood marks on the wall, sand and pebbles.

DI Morris collected, from the Pathologist, as much information from the girl's trendy handbag as he could. The Home Office official was able to give him the personal details to enable him to speak to the family of the dead girl. She and her family had moved locally only a matter of a couple of weeks before this tragedy. DI Morris immediately visited the parents with a female police constable. They did not mention at this time that rape had been committed after death. It was all too shocking for a parent to hear.

The Detective Inspector was called to the Mortuary at about 1700 and was told of the horrific circumstances surrounding the brutal attack on the young girl. He was shown the bruises on her body and was told of the reasons why the Forensic Team thought the rape happened after death. The only evidence they had was a sample of the man's semen which would only prove the man's blood group, which was the common blood group O Rhesus Negative.

Even for an experienced DI it made Neil's stomach churn. He vowed that he would catch this man but realised he had little to go on. He had managed to get a photograph of the young girl from her parents.

He started by organising the questioning of all the residents of Marine Parade, Piermont Place and Brookdale Terrace, then the landlords of the local pubs. Several constables were walking around the town talking to holiday makers as well as local people and several more officers were outside the pubs to question anyone that was out the night before. One police officer was told to speak to the four local doctors to ask them for names and addresses of local men with O Rhesus Positive blood group.

The list was huge so the sergeant started right away knocking on the front doors of the possible rapists.

The DI decided to stay in the town and managed to secure a room at the Charlton House Hotel on a B & B basis. The accommodation was clean and nicely decorated. The large window overlooked the sea and the bottom of the town where the shocking incident had happened.

He flopped down onto the bed deep in thought about the young girl, whilst running his fingers through his blond hair. He was determined to catch this man. He had already had a Constable who had spoken to the porters and ticket staff at the railway station and had another Constable questioning the bus drivers and conductors who were on duty that night. Road blocks were set up at the top of Teignmouth Hill and also at the top of Iddesleigh Terrace to ask the drivers and passengers if they had any information they could share.

It took a week of relentless questioning and the feeling of getting nowhere before Neil Morris decided to go for an off duty drink in the town. He walked down the main Exeter Road to the South Devon Inn. He found it very pleasant and the landlord recognised him instantly.

"What can I get you?" said Phil the landlord.

"Pint of your best please" replied Neil.

"Coming up and on the house" Phil added.

The conversation continued, Phil never asked any questions, he just mooted how difficult the police's work must be. Neil appreciated that. He wanted to talk to locals and hoped that someone, somewhere would have just something that he could work on. There was only a couple of elderly men in the bar so he asked the landlord if that was normal trade.

"Only on a Monday night. We usually hold dart, snooker and skittles matches in the back room during the week and the local branch of the Buffalos (the men only charitable organisation) hold their weekly meetings on a Friday night, but whether all that will continue during this time - who knows? The town is in shock, things like that just do not happen here" Phil replied.

"Well that's it for tonight, must get my beauty sleep I have a busy day tomorrow. See you soon, Phil".

Neil realised that in a small town like this, people would be worried about going out especially the ladies. He decided to call it a night.

"Night, Neil"

The next day he deployed his team of Constables to the streets again to ask and answer questions from the public. They had orders to report directly to him if anyone had any information at all regarding the murder of the young girl.

The following night he decided to try the other pubs. The Gresham had only a few older men sat around the bar. They were all very pleasant but could offer no information. The landlord mentioned that this was about the limit of his Tuesday night trade so Neil thought he would move on to the next pub.

He only had to look towards the bottom of the steps across the road to see the Railway Inn. He walked in and found the landlord puffing on his pipe talking to a very elderly gentleman sitting at the bar.

"Welcome to the Railway Inn, what would you like to drink, sir" said the landlord.

"A pint of your best, please".

"Aren't you the top brass from London running the murder enquiry in the town?" Said the old man who had turned in his stool to face Neil.

"Yes, I am. I have decided to stay in Dawlish, pretty little place. There doesn't seem to be many people about, is that normal?" asked Neil.

"This is like a winter night" said the Landlord "Our dart team are playing the Swan Inn tonight, that's at the back of the town, some will come back for a last minute pint, but apart from that we will be quiet – especially now there has been a murder. Any nearer finding this maniac?"

"Unfortunately, no".

Neil decided to drink up and go back to the Charlton House Hotel. When he got back to the hotel he found that the bar was still open but, like most places, there was a definite lack of customers and was very quiet. He sat and chatted to the barman for half an hour then decided to take a drink back to his room. The barman was very polite, he said he couldn't help with the enquiries, he was working the night of the murder and also didn't know very many locals in town because his job was a 'live in' situation. He continued to write his list for the next day's brewery order.

Neil decided to strike the barman's name off of the list of possible suspects he could always get his rota from the Manager if needed.

After nearly a week with still no leads, Neil decided to go to the local pubs and beaches at the weekend. He strolled down the town and walked over to Coryton Cove. There were loads of people there and really some nice looking young women. He bought lunch from the little cafe and decided to sit on the small wall on the top of the slope. It was a beautiful day and the sunshine reflecting on the water interjected by swimmers was such a tonic. The sea gulls flying low over the beach and their screams and clucking made it all seem just like any other holiday resort. A peregrine falcon that was nesting on the red sandstone cliffs above the cove soared above the throng of people and the children were running about screaming and getting excited about sand castles and ice cream. Even in the rock pools the children and adults were having innocent fun. It cheered Neil, who thought he was in heaven after leaving the London suburb that he had called home for all of his 40 years.

His thoughts were interrupted by the sight of three young women coming up the slope. Laura, a blonde with a fabulous figure, the second girl Susan, was a very pretty dark haired girl, a bit shorter than the first, the third was a brown haired girl looking fabulous in a red and white spotted bikini. All three had good figures and good all over tans. Andy thought they looked like contestant from a beauty pageant. He was very interested in all three.

CHAPTER SIXTEEN

A few months later, when he thought the reactions of the rape of the young girl had subsided, the prisoner decided he would take a chance of the police not being around so much, he decided to go for a swim - the weather was just perfect. He went to Coastguards beach, the water was chilly at first, but after a while his body got used to the temperature and the escapee was able to completely unwind. The sun was still shining and he was feeling good. He wasn't handsome but he had a good body. He had been, when working in the garden, taking his shirt off and working in his 'new' swimming trunks so he had quite a good tan and his muscles were well toned.

He leant against the sea wall in the sunshine to dry off. His grubby towel was only used to get dressed under. Another lone male swimmer started to speak to him, he sounded quite pleasant.

"The sea is still a little chilly isn't it?" He heard him say.

"Yes, but we can't have everything, the water is clean here and the sun is still shining" he replied.

"They say the weather is going to stay hot for another week" said the thick set man.

"Hope so, I love the summer. I am not really interested in football, much prefer a swim and spend time on the beach" said the prisoner.

"I agree, I am going for a pint, do you fancy one, there's a nice little pub just under the viaduct, plenty of pretty young women there" he replied with a smile on his face.

How could he refuse? A free man going for a drink in a pub. He replied "Yes" instantly.

The bar was busy and friendly, all talk was still of the rape and murder on the beach in the town. The thick set swimmer started to talk to a good looking dark haired young man as the escapee recognised a young woman – it was the girl he had flashed to and the girl who he thought had the stones. He couldn't take his eyes off of her, she had matured into a very attractive young lady and he wanted her now. She didn't look his way at all she was too interested in talking and laughing with her girlfriends.

He thought 'Just bide your time with this one, just bide your time'!

When the prisoner's new friend returned from the bar, the strange thick set swimmer told him that the chap he had been talking to, Matt Thackery, was the owner of the caravan who he shared with, just on a temporary basis. He needed somewhere to live as he had been thrown out of his lodgings. He had come to Dawlish from Cornwall looking for work and a local builder in the pub offered him a labourer's job on a building site. Matt Thackery being a kind hearted person, offered him temporary lodgings at his caravan at Dawlish Warren. He added that he hadn't met his girlfriend yet, but she was the pretty girl wearing an orange coloured dress, talking to Matt.

What Matt and the builder did not know was that his story was mostly lies. He did come from Bodmin Moor in Cornwall but just over seven years ago. The true story was that he had served the seven years in Exeter prison because he was caught growing marijuana at his parent's small holding. A young off duty policewoman, who was walking on the moor with her boyfriend, recognised the plant and after she reported it the police found that he had previous history for growing drugs in one of his parent's barn.

When the police raided the property very early one morning, they found more plants than they had realised. They also managed to ascertain that he was a peddler of the drug in Plymouth. He realised that he had been rumbled and he took it out on the police. He came out of his room with a 12 bore shotgun and aimed it at the police, then fired at the first person who moved, wounding the policewomen in the leg. He was charged with attempted murder, resisting arrest and growing and selling an illegal drug. He was charged at Exeter Crown Court and went straight to prison.

He served a full 7 years and, when released, had nowhere to go, his parents had both died in prison where they were serving their sentences, he had no brothers, sisters or relatives and the farm had belonged to a local estate so was only being rented by his parents.

*   *   *   *   *

After listening to his new friend, the escapee settled back into his chair at the pub so that Georgina couldn't see him from where she was standing.

'So, this Matt is her boyfriend' thought the prisoner. 'Well, well, I wonder if my new swimming pal would tell me their plans, he's already told me half of his life! I want to get the stones back from her – they are mine. I wonder if the muscular swimmer could be bribed. I will have to go to London to get a good price from Smokey Joe for those stones. Hopefully Smokey would still be in the East End of London'.

Neil walked into the pub and was recognised by the landlord straight away, but having such a busy pub Ernie, the landlord, had known for years to keep quiet about the police, he could lose a lot of the new customers that he didn't know. He was a law abiding citizen and would always help if needed but it was in his own interest to respect the confidentiality of the officer.

"Good evening, what would you like a drink?"

"Pint of your best bitter, please" replied Neil.

Neil stood at the bar and tried to look at all the characters, he missed quite a few people because the room was so full of drinkers. There was a mixture of ages from, he would guess, barely drinking age to pensioners but everyone was getting on with each other. All the talk was of the young girl found on the beach. He thought they were all a little sombre – not even the juke box was on, they all seemed genuinely caring people. It was just the right place for rumours to get completely out of hand. Neil knew his constables would be busy answering questions on the streets of Dawlish the next day.

The questions he was desperate to get answers to were, who was the murdered girl going to visit, or had she already visited them, or was she meeting someone at the bus stop? He felt he might find out this information in a pub – people talk when they have had a few to drink or maybe he would find out tomorrow.

His thoughts came to a stop when, through the throng of people, he noticed the girl in the orange dress. She had been one of the three girls on the beach, the one with the brown hair. Suddenly the gang of young men blocking his view drank up and left the pub. He then noticed the other two girls from the beach who were sitting at the long table by the window. The girl in the orange dress was talking to a good looking young man with dark hair. The other two girls were chatting to several other girls and a few young men standing close by. They were all very attractive girls and Neil, although a little older than them, thought he might try his luck.

He stood at the bar and listened to the conversations of the customers, it was always about the murder of the young girl. He was also waiting for the chance to speak to the girl with brown hair. The man she had been talking to decided to go across the lane to the gents and left her talking to a ruddy faced young man called Tom from, it sounded to Neil like Ashcombe, but he wasn't sure about that because of the noise from the other drinkers. Neil didn't wait even a second and moved closer and started talking to her before Matt had reached the door.

"Hello, it's busy in here tonight, are you local?" said Neil.

Georgina, wondered who this handsome, sophisticated, stranger was, and replied "Yes, I am, born and bred. Haven't seen you in here before".

"No, it's my first time, have only been in Dawlish for a few weeks, nice place".

"Apart from the murder" she replied.

"Did you know her?" Neil asked.

"No, I understand she had only lived here for a while. I have been living in London for two years". She replied.

"Oh, that's where I come from, what part?"

"I work in Putney, but live with relatives in Battersea" she said as she looked towards the door and saw Matt returning.

Matt looked and saw Georgina talking to the stranger and made his way through the throng of people and stood beside her. Matt was immediately aware that he had a rival.

"What is your name?" The detective asked Georgina.

"Georgina" she replied.

She looked at him and thought he was very attractive, quite a bit older than her but seemed very worldly wise, interesting and intelligent.

Matt interrupted the conversation by saying to Georgina "It's time we were going".

Georgina just had time to drink the last of her drink, say goodbye to Tom, as she was rushed out of the pub to go to the Grand Hotel.

"Georgina, you really must be more careful, no-one seemed to know that chap, he could be the murderer" Matt said as they walked down Fishy lane. "He seemed a nice chap, I didn't think, sorry" replied Georgina.

When 'Last Orders' were rang, the escapee didn't want his new friend to know where he was living so he made the excuse that he was going home in the opposite direction to where his new mate lived. He made up his mind the new friend was a little thick because he told him exactly where he lived. It was easy for the escapee to point in the other direction.

He kept going in the unknown direction for quite a while, he followed the brook up as far as the Manor gardens. It was a very dark night and he had had several pints of cider but his night vision was still good, so he was surprised when he came across a young woman walking a little Yorkshire terrier. No-one else was around.

Prisoner 1852 couldn't believe his luck, he managed to creep silently on the grass verge beside the concrete path, and when behind her he put his hands around her face, covering her mouth, she struggled but, not only was he a lot stronger than her, he had his Swiss army knife which he put against her throat. She felt the tip of the knife and knew exactly what it was, she was terrified and so frightened she couldn't do a thing to help herself. He managed to pull her into a large rhododendron bush and put his hand up her mini skirt quickly and easily.

A small low growing branch that had been broken started to dig into her back like a bayonet and with the weight of this ugly man on top of her, she found it was very painful. The small rooted branch had started to push its way through her skin and with the movement of his continuous thrusting made the branch go further into her body. She screamed in agony.

"Please leave me alone, you're hurting me" she sobbed.

He was enjoying listening to her pleading but the loud high pitched shrieking was making him very agitated, although he knew his roughness towards her body was making the pain far worse, it didn't stop him.

"You're hurting me" she cried.

"Shut up, bitch" was his reply.

It was all over in a matter of minutes. The dog, who was still at the end of the lead which was looped over her hand, was shaking and howling inside the bush. Somehow in the struggle the dog had been kicked. The ugly man kicked him again, this time in the head, with a single yelp the dog fell silent forever.

The prisoner casually made his way downstream feeling smug and satisfied. He made his way back to the beach and quickly walked up Elm Grove Road. Later when he was back in the safety of the garden, he thought that when he knew his new swimming friend better, when he could trust him, he may tell him about Georgina and the stones, he felt sure he could be bribed, he would be able to get information from the boyfriend about her. He never gave the lady in the Manor gardens another thought - he had had what he wanted.

He lay in his bed and thought about the only thing he needed now was a woman a couple of times a week. He was thinking about Georgina as well. Thinking that she wasn't too young now. He would have her, he would definitely have her.

'Next week, I will have another one if not HER' he promised himself.

He fell asleep thinking about Georgina. He was angry with her for taking and hiding the jewels from him but he fancied her and felt he could forgive her and adorn her with the jewels if she were to give herself to him. He tossed and turned in the bed dreaming about her and woke with a start.

'Why is she getting under my skin? Why am I going soft with her? I mustn't do that – that is just ridiculous for me to be soft over a woman – won't be long before I go soft over a dog!' He thought.

CHAPTER SEVENTEEN

The next morning, a ten year old boy and his sister who was six were playing in the Manor gardens when they found the bloodied body of the local lady and the body of the dog. They ran home to their parents and quickly garbled out what they had found. The father went to the large bush to check their story then he went into the Manor House and informed the council and asked them to phone the police, he then stood outside the bush to stop others from seeing this awful sight. The children's mother gave the children cups of hot sweet tea then sat on the settee and cuddled them, they were in complete shock. The little girl started to cry and her brother was exceptionally quiet. It wasn't long before the ambulance and police cars went at full speed to the Manor Gardens.

DI Neil Morris arrived on the scene soon after. The same Forensic Scientist that had dealt with the body of the young girl on the beach arrived just after him. The Detective was shocked to think there was another murder in this small nice town. The young woman had no identification on her so DI Morris guessed that, as no-one had reported her missing the night before she must live on her own.

The father, who had checked inside the bush recognised the body and told the policeman on duty. She had been living locally for several years, she was a neighbour of his family and lived in a cottage across the road from the gardens.

The Police had cordoned off the gardens and posted a policeman at every entrance into the Manor grounds, then the Home Office Pathologist arrived. He informed Neil that he would phone him after his examination at the Mortuary.

Neil, although an experienced officer, rubbed his hands through his hair as if he was at a loss as to where to start this investigation. He had absolutely nothing to go on. He took his time to carefully interview the children who were still very upset over the sight of their neighbour. Neil didn't press them too much, he basically just asked them if they saw anyone, either a complete stranger or local person before they went into the bush or after they came out. They both just stared into space and almost whispered the negative reply that Neil was dreading.

After several hours the Pathologist gave Neil a door key that was in her pocket and, after the children's father showed him where she lived Neil went, with a police Sergeant and a Constable, into her cottage. There was no-one in the two up two down home. It was very clean and tidy and was obviously inhabited by a lone person. He asked the two men to thoroughly search the cottage and to specifically look for paperwork regarding who she was and possible next of kin, also any recent photographs of anyone, male or female.

He went back in his mind to his training. He had to speak to family, neighbours and friends after interviewing eye witnesses - but there were no eye witnesses! He positioned all of his constables and officers strategically around the town and did everything he could possibly do to get a lead, no matter how small, but nothing was forthcoming.

DI Neil Morris had decided to rent a flat in the town and stay until called back by the Met. He wanted to see Georgina again and was disappointed to hear that she had gone back to London and hoped she would be back by Christmas at least.

The one person missing that no-one realised was the ugly man. He thought it may be better if he stayed low for several months. The weather turned very wet and cold and he seemed to suffer with repeated chest infections, all he had to fight it was Aspirin and a bottle of brandy. He had never had chest problems before until he spent those cold, wet nights sleeping rough when he first escaped from Dartmoor, so he decided to stay in the warmth of his bed in his living shed. His stocky friend had no idea where he lived so he knew he would not be disturbed.

It was lucky he did stay low after the second rape and killing because Neil had been given extra budget and personnel, some were very experienced detectives, to help with the search for the killer. He had also been given the use of a large room in the Manor House for use as an Incident Room. He was grateful for that because the extra staff were falling over each other in the small room at the Dawlish Police Station in Park Road. Extra desks and filing cabinets arrived shortly after moving to the new room. A telephone engineer was also sent to set up several new lines. He was also given a smaller room for himself with a secretary on loan from the Exeter Headquarters.

Neil already knew he was dealing with a dangerous serial offender, so he was not too shocked when told, during that conversation with the Pathologist, that the semen found on the bodies of the girl on the beach and the lady in the Manor gardens were from a man with the same blood group, O Rhesus Negative, the chances being it would be the same man. Also that the cause of death on the second victim was the branch that dug into her back had gone into a main artery, hence the amount of blood loss. He would write in his report:-

'CAUSE OF DEATH – SHARP FORCE INJURY'

CHAPTER EIGHTEEN

Georgina had her return train ticket to go back to London in her hand. Matt had driven her to the station. They were both very upset at the thought that they wouldn't see each other for another three months.

"Never mind, we can make up for it at Christmas" said Georgina.

His reply pleased her "Yes, we will have the best Christmas yet, and you can wear the engagement ring I am going to buy you".

"Yes please" she said as she hugged him close to her. He kissed her and told her he loved her with all his heart.

Just as the train was pulling into the station a local lad approached them and told them that another woman had been raped and murdered and was found in the Manor gardens the night before.

"Thank God you are getting out of this town for a while. I will phone you at your Aunts tonight and let you know all the information about the murdered woman. Please take care Georgina and don't be too trusting of strangers, remember I love you very much".

The noise of the steam coming out of the engine finished the conversation as Georgina kissed him goodbye then boarded the train for the four hour journey to Paddington.

"See you at Christmas" she shouted hoping that he heard her.

She felt he looked quite sad as she waved him goodbye, she was close to tears and decided to try to make this the last time she ever leaves him. It was with a very heavy heart when she found an empty seat and sat down.

Georgina's new position at work was very interesting and busy. Colin and the other members of the small department were super, good fun and, when not in the office, social drinkers. They all went into the pub, close to the office, most evenings. In the main, they only stayed for about an hour. It made sense really, as Colin explained, they miss the rush hour.

Georgina and Colin went to the pub with Brenda, Phillis, Bill, Roy and a very funny, highly intelligent chap called Ian from South Africa. They were all such good fun, which Georgina felt she needed at that time.

Another week had gone by and Colin had said that another three months then they should be finished writing the encyclopaedia. He added that after that time any errors could be recorded if and when they happened.

"Don't worry Georgina, we will always find you another position" he said.

Georgina thought long and hard about this news and, although she had not been thinking of Matt so often, she still loved him deeply and thought it a good way to say goodbye to Simon. She would go home.

She spoke to Stuart Barrington, her Line Manager.

"I think it is time I went back to Devon, Stuart. Would it be possible to give in my notice now, then leave when the project has finished?"

"Yes, of course, are you sure that is what you want? We will obviously miss you, but to be honest we all know we will be looking for new jobs in a couple of months' time. This department is definitely moving to Reading by summer. I will personally give you an excellent reference.

"Thank you Stuart".

Every time Georgina and her colleagues went to the pub after work, it was as if the department was splitting up immediately, it always finished up like a party. Deep down, they were all quite upset about it as they all got on so well.

Telling Simon she was leaving London went a lot better than she thought.

"I will miss you sweetheart. Do you really want to go?" he said after the initial shock was over.

"Yes, I think the time is right".

They both realised that, although they thought the world of each other, there could never be anything more than that because of their differing views on several major issues especially politics.   They promised to remain close friends and accepted that they would meet now and then if she came back to London or if he went on holiday to Dawlish.

The move back to Devon was delayed for about three months because of the work that needed to be done in the office. Most were pleased with this situation, the hour at the pub after work was always extended to sometimes as late as 10pm.

Georgina was really excited about the Christmas holidays, she had two weeks off of work and told Matt, when he rang, that she would come back to

Dawlish for good at the end of March. It was disappointing but she couldn't let her bosses down, they had always been so good to her. Matt understood this and just accepted the situation.

Christmas Eve at the Exeter Inn was an ideal time to tell everyone that they had got engaged, the large single diamond ring fitted perfectly. Ernie had bottles of champagne on ice and her family were there as well as Matt's Mum and Dad. They were surrounded by friends wishing them good luck. The celebrations continued in the Grand Hotel with everyone enjoying a chicken in a basket supper, dancing and singing.

A few days after the New Year Georgina had to travel back to London for the extra three months. She was surprised when she saw Neil at the railway station. Matt was not pleased. If it had not been for the fact that he had to take his mum and dad to an uncle's funeral the next day he would have bought a ticket and gone to London with her.

They boarded the train and Neil sat beside her. As she waved goodbye to her handsome man through the train window Matt noticed that Neil had a smug look on his face. He thought he was goading him. He didn't like the big headed stranger and wouldn't trust him at all.

Georgina felt sorry for Matt and wanted to tell him that she would never hurt his feelings or antagonise him in any way and she wanted to tell him that right now, but the train was pulling out of the station.

During the journey Neil told her that he was taking a fortnight's annual leave he felt he needed a break. Someone else from London was going to take his place in Dawlish just for the two weeks. He asked Georgina if they might meet up and go to see a show or something while they were both in the city.

Once again she saw him in a good light. He was attractive, he had a good sense of humour and, although quite a bit older than her, he was able to speak on many topics that a twenty year old would, the latest fashions, whatever song was number one in the charts, the best groups and all kinds of up-to-date knowledge. She found him exceptionally attractive, both mentally and physically and whenever there was a lull in the conversation, she would look out of the window and imagined him making love to her, but would never admit to that.

The only worry to Georgina was that he kept asking personal questions about Matt. She was very careful with her answers.

They arrived at Paddington Station and Neil suggested they share a taxi, he told her that his home was quite close to where she lived.

As she was getting out of the taxi outside her aunt and uncle's house, he said "I will pay the fare and pick you up tomorrow night at 7 o'clock. Drive on driver".

She didn't get a chance to even say goodbye or say "Yes" or "No" to the date, as the taxi moved down the road and out of sight quickly.

Feeling angry with him for presuming she would go on this date, she carried her suitcase to the door wondering if she should meet him as suggested.

She kept thinking of Matt telling her not to trust this man, who she knew nothing about.

After making a cup of tea she sat and thought about this date. She didn't want to upset Matt, she was now engaged but would Neil make life difficult for her and Matt back in Dawlish if she didn't go. He will be back home before me, would he tell lies about her to Matt. Georgina decided not to go but she would tell Matt when he phoned that evening. Or should she not tell him, she didn't want to cause trouble.

The tea was soon changed to gin and Georgina decided not to say anything to Matt, she would deal with this on her own.

The next day she made her way to the office and arrived before anyone else. They gradually came in blaming the traffic chaos. Her colleagues were all delighted with her news of the engagement and decided that was an excuse for a drink in the pub after work. Brenda and Phyllis felt that something was wrong and asked Georgina if she was ok.

Georgina told them of the rapes and murders in Dawlish and also of the Detective Inspector and his idea of her wanting to go out with him. Their advice was for her to be at home tonight when he called and to tell him straight that she was not interested in him.

The doorbell rang at just before 7 o'clock and Georgina went to answer it. She was in her jeans and a jumper. It was Neil. He was shocked to think that she was turning him down. Most of his adult life he had had his own way and was so arrogant that he never thought a woman would refuse to go out with him.

"The taxi went off so quickly that I couldn't explain to you why I wouldn't be joining you tonight. As you know I have just got engaged to Matt, who I love dearly, and would never be unfaithful to him. Not only that I didn't have your phone number to contact you. Sorry you have had a wasted journey" She said.

"Not to worry Georgina, just come to the pub at the end of the road and have a drink with me?"

'What harm could it do' thought the very naïve Georgina.

When they found a table in the bar of the very old pub, Neil quickly made Georgina feel at ease and using his experience with women he was able to show his interesting and humorous side. She didn't need to ask him about his private life he was willing to tell her – she believed him straight away. It never entered her head that he was telling her lies and that he had a wife and two children living in London.

What he did tell her was that he was divorced and lonely.

She fell for his charm and when he walked her home, he was the perfect gentleman. He kissed her goodnight passionately and lovingly at the front door of her aunt's house, she tried to resist but found that she was really enjoying his embrace. He asked if she would like to go, just as friends, to the opera on Thursday night to see La Boheme. She agreed readily.

"I will pick you up at 6 o'clock – we can grab something to eat after the performance".

She went indoors and closed the door.

For the rest of the week, she felt wretched. She thought she would never, ever, be unfaithful to Matt but why did she felt guilty about just going for a drink with another man? Georgina kept saying to herself 'pull yourself together, it is just a bit of fun, companionship. It won't be long before I am in Matts arms for ever.'

Thursday night arrived and Georgina had decided to wear her little black dress which she thought was acceptable for an opera. Neil was on time, he drove and parked close to Leicester Square then they walked to the Theatre.

"Neil, you must let me go Dutch on this evening".

"Certainly not, I would not dream of letting a lady pay her way". He said this quite sternly.

"Well thank you" she said, not wanting to upset him by insisting she help pay.

It was the first time Georgina had been to an opera. She really did enjoy it. They managed to get a drink and a meal after the performance in a restaurant near Leicester Square and talked, not just about the opera, but about worldly things, news from abroad and politics in general. There was no one party hate or nasty discussion of Ministers which Georgina was thankful for.

When Neil was driving her home, he started talking about her future life back in Dawlish. He was asking whether she would be happy without the social life of London, the shops, cinemas, theatres. He also asked whether she would be happy with Matt.

Georgina was feeling a little light headed after the couple of cocktails she had had that evening so she managed to completely ignore his questions and turned it around to telling him her plans to travel after marriage.

They arrived in the road where she lived and sat in the car talking about travelling.

"I cannot offer you the Seychelles but do you fancy going to Brighton on Saturday?" he asked.

"Brighton?" she giggled "What for and how long does it take?"

"It only takes just over an hour to get there, I am thinking of buying a cottage by the sea and I have arranged for a viewing on Saturday afternoon, I could do with your feminine views"

"OK" she replied.

His kisses were passionate and Georgina found herself enjoying every minute of the closeness that they shared together when he was wrapping himself around her.

"Pick you up on Saturday morning about 9 o'clock. Goodnight darling".

Georgina went indoors and quickly went to bed. She found it difficult to sleep because Neil's words about her imminent return to Dawlish and the different lifestyle that she had mapped out for herself was sinking in.

She was having thoughts that she never dreamed she would ever have. Would she really be happy living with Matt? Would she be happy with someone who has never lived outside of Dawlish? Would she eventually find him boring? Why was Neil appearing in her thoughts more than Matt as she lay in her little single bed? Why did she find Neil so irresistible?

*　　*　　*　　*　　*

On the Saturday morning she got up really early thinking a cup of tea might make her feel better. The weather was cloudy and cold so she dressed herself with her favourite jeans, boots and a warm jumper and coat. Neil picked her up in his car about 10 minutes before 9 o'clock. As it was a Saturday the traffic on the roads was not too heavy. When they arrived in Brighton their first stop was to the beach which was covered with pebbles, very windy and freezing cold. They made their way to a coffee shop and had a big fried breakfast, when they felt warmer they ran to the pier. A stroll along the windy promenade passed the time.

They found the empty cottage down a narrow road only minutes from the beach. From the outside, Georgina thought it was lovely but she was put off when they met with the Estate Agent and Neil introduced her as the 'future Mrs Morris'. Everything he said was a pack of lies regarding their relationship. She showed no interest in the property or him, she just wanted to go home.

"I would like to go home, Neil" she stammered when the Estate Agent had left them.

"Well I am not going home just yet, and the last train has gone" he replied.

"What harm has been done, I am hungry, let's find somewhere to eat and drink".

Eventually they found a back street pub that was clean and welcoming. They ordered dinner and she had the opportunity to question him about his behaviour in front of the Agent.

"Why did you tell so many lies about us?" she asked.

"Just thought I would" he replied arrogantly.

She found this very strange but he had been plying her with gin all evening and she felt so happy, warm and tingly. She was now over 20 years old and had managed to stop men having their sexual pleasures with her, now everything seemed different. She was still a virgin and had promised herself to keep pure for Matt. Now she was not so sure and the way she was feeling she couldn't have cared less.

When she came back from the ladies toilet she found Neil was getting drunker by the minute about half an hour later she found that her speech was slow and her head was feeling woolly. It was Georgina who decided that they should stay for the night in a room at the pub as he was certainly not capable of driving. They laughed and joked as they both stumbled up the stairs, Neil found it difficult to carry two glasses and a bottle of wine. He filled the glasses full while Georgina went to the bathroom which was down the hallway.

When Neil came back from his visit to the toilet, Georgina was stretched across the bed with all her clothes on and only her shoes off. Neil found this exciting and pounced on her, she started giggling and was responsive to his fantasies when undressing her. Because he was an older, more experienced man, he knew how to please a woman. She found his touch tender and his experienced lovemaking, which was so new to her, took her to heights she never knew existed.

They woke at six o'clock and it was then that Georgina realised what she had done. When she stood up, she felt as if she was suffering from Vertigo, her head was whizzing around and she had a funny muzzled noise coming from her ears, she felt as if she was drowning. She was also feeling very guilty that she had not kept herself for Matt. She quickly washed and dressed and was ready to travel back to London immediately.

During the journey back to London, the fuzziness in Georgina's head was beginning to subside. The memories of the night before was coming back to her. Did she really go to bed with a man that she hardly knew, she doubted that it was drink that made her feel so bad she was always able to take her drink. Surely he didn't put something in her drink that made her feel ill? Although she did enjoy what he had done to her, she was feeling guilty and ashamed. She hardly spoke to him until they arrived at her aunt's house.

"What's the matter, have I said something that has upset you?"

"No, I just feel very guilty about two timing Matt. How can I face him now" was her pathetic reply.

He wasn't very understanding and just said "Didn't you enjoy it? I know I did. It was a bit of fun".

Hearing that response Georgina felt dirty and used. She didn't reply to what he said she felt as if she would burst into tears. She never, ever wanted to see him again.

"Come on Georgina, surely in this day and age you weren't expecting us to stay there without sex? What did you think the day was all about? You must admit you enjoyed it?" he said then added "You came to Brighton with me voluntary, you are over 16 years of age and if I remember rightly, you were the one who suggested we stay the night in the pub, so legally it was your instigation, I have done nothing wrong, we can still see each other in Dawlish when you come back".

"How long are you staying in Dawlish?" she demanded, realising that she had no idea that was his plan.

"I like it so much, if I can get a transfer to the Devon and Cornwall Constabulary, I will stay forever" he said as he was looking for her reaction.

She understood quite well what he was doing and was disgusted with herself and that she was so naïve.

"Don't think for one minute that I will give Matt up. Last night was a mistake, and I have known him long enough to know that he will forgive me. I will phone him tonight to tell him what I have done. You have yet to learn that

Dawlish people know one another's history, so no-one would believe you, you would not be liked " she was choking back the tears as she was stammering these words out.

He obviously didn't like her reply and just replied "I am a respected Detective Inspector, would people believe you and Matt or me?"

"You obviously have a lot to learn in Dawlish Matt and I would be believed before a stranger, police or no police" she quickly replied.

"Perhaps I should put that to the test when I go back to Dawlish next week" he bellowed.

CHAPTER NINETEEN

When the department eventually closed Georgina found it quite upsetting. She knew she would miss Simon, warts and all, her aunt, uncle and her cousins, all her friends at work – but she knew she must move on. She was now more interested in loving Matt for ever. She hoped she would be able to forget Brighton and would tell Matt when she thought the time was right.

Georgina arrived back in Dawlish and was looking forward to the summer. For a couple of days everything was idyllic. Matt was looking good, he was so pleased she was home. Georgina felt so guilty about her trip to Brighton with Neil, so was pleased when it appeared that Matt obviously knew nothing about their one night stand. She had thoughts of telling him, she knew she must.

Georgina took the bus, as soon as possible, to Teignmouth to sign on the dole, mainly so that she could sit on the beach all through those glorious hot months to come, but they offered her a position in an office in Exeter.

A week later on the bus going home from the interview in Exeter she realised she must do something about the stones, the ugly man and now whether to tell Matt about her indiscretion with the policeman.

Unfortunately, when Georgina arrived home at her mother's house, she received the news from her sister, Eileen, that Matt had been taken in for questioning of the two rapes and murders at the Incident Rooms in the Manor House. She phoned Matt's mum and found that the story was true and that his Dad was with him at the incident room.

Georgina quickly grabbed her jacket and rushed down Stockton Hill towards the Manor. She saw the Receptionist and asked whether she could see Matt Thackeray.

"If you would like to take a seat, I will find out for you".

She showed Georgina into a tiny room with seats round the walls. Mr Thackeray was already there waiting to speak to him.

"Hello Georgina, thank you for coming, I really do not know why they suspect Matt" he said.

"Don't worry, I can verify where he was on those nights" replied Georgina.

"I have been keeping a five year diary and I know that we were at Rene's party at The Smugglers Inn, it was a private party celebrating her birthday and we didn't leave there until the early hours there were about 30 people, so lots of locals including Rene and her family would remember us being there.

The night of the second murder, we were at the Exeter Inn talking to the Detective Inspector who is running this investigation, she shuddered when she thought of that. Hopefully Neil, she thought, would deny all knowledge of their conversation, but Ernie, Laura and Susan would remember. After that we went to the Grand Hotel with two of my friends and we were sat with a couple of friends of Matt's Mum and Dad, who are both solicitors".

An hour later, Matt came out of the temporary Interview Room and told Georgina and Mr Thackeray that he had not been charged but was told not to leave his parent's home until told he can. He was still under suspicion of rape and murder.

"Can I speak to Neil Morris?" said Georgina to the receptionist.

"Just one moment, I will see if he is available. Can I take your name?"

"Georgina Cartwright"

She came back from the Incident Room "DI Morris is not available at this time, he has asked that you call back another day".

Georgina found this infuriating but managed to hold her temper for fear of letting something slip and Matt finding out about her dalliance.

They decided to go to his parent's house for a cup of tea.

Mrs Thackeray was in such a state that Georgina went into the kitchen and made the tea. When she returned to the sitting room she found them all in tears.

She went to Matt first and he said "You don't think I did it do you?"

"Of course not Matt, anyway we can prove where we were on those nights, I looked at my diary before I left home. We were at Rene's party the night of the first murder, then the second we were talking to Neil Morris in the Exeter Inn and then we had drinks with your mum and dad's friends in the Grand Hotel. Do you remember?"

"Yes I do, but didn't realise it was on those two nights. Oh, Georgina, you are so good for me, I will love you forever".

Feeling a massive guilt trip, Georgina felt very humble, she realised that she had done wrong, why had she been so stupid to even think that anyone could be better than Matt?"

"Oh, thank God for your diary, but don't forget I rushed you out of there because I wanted to get you away from Neil Morris" he said.

They all seemed to be happier knowing that they had witnesses as to Matt's whereabouts.   His dad gave Georgina a lift home.

When Georgina went to bed, she was worrying about this turn of events as to why Neil has decided to take this out on Matt. 'I thought I had explained to Neil that I should never have slept with him. Was he that hurt? Surely a man like him would not be so heartless.'

She also knew she must check that the stones were still inside Pandy. She thought she should go straight to the police – but not at this time with Matt being held on suspicion of murder and especially not to Neil Morris.   If she had been acting against the law all this time – he would not believe her and she would definitely lose her job opportunity to become a Civil Servant. She was now in a state and she really didn't know what to do.

On the Friday night in Dawlish she met up with the girls and went into the Exeter Inn. It wasn't long before Matt came in.

"You look really well" she said to him.

"So do you maid. Neil Morris has finally dropped me from the suspects list" he said.

"Was it him that arrested you?"

"Yes, the crummy little bastard, I never did like him and most of the men in the 'Exeter' don't like him either. Tom Hunt reckons he is one of the worst kind of policemen because he is so righteous and thinks we are all thick in Dawlish. We are all wondering why we have to put up with him".

Oh, Matt, nobody we know would suspect you, what evidence did he have?

"Obviously none"

"Well, it really is good news I do love you very much - please just try to put it behind you. My good news is that I already have had an interview for a job with the Civil Service in Exeter I think it went well so fingers crossed, then I hopefully can spend the summer weekends on the beach".

Georgina felt he looked much better than he had looked for several years.

"I still love you very much, I am so pleased you are home, you have made me very happy. I have been worried about you for ages, in fact years" he said.

She thought she knew that he would try to get her into bed but this time she was wrong, it was different. Was it because he didn't drink so much? He had got older? Or was it because she really wanted him?

He drove to Haldon, told her again that he loved her very much. They sat in the car listening to Radio Luxemburg and talked of the future. Although Matt wanted to settle down - get married, buy a house in Dawlish, and have a couple of children, Georgina was keen to travel, while they were still young. Georgina explained that the world was beginning to open up to everybody, not just the rich and famous. They discussed this at length and decided to get married, buy a house, rent it out then travel for about two years. They spoke of travelling around Europe first, preferably by local transport, then going further afield as and when they chose. It sounded idyllic. Matt soon came around to the idea.

"Just imagine swimming in the Indian Ocean, travelling to Australia and New Zealand" he said, he was getting excited just thinking about it.

She was so pleased that he was keen to do the same. "It could be great fun, but we must be careful the world is a big place and not everyone is a kind soul, there are a lot of rogues out there".

At 2am the radio station closed down. Every night the final song was an old hymn, it was a beautiful hymn which they sang together.

"This will be our song" he said romantically.

"Oh, Matt that's beautiful".

The whole evening was wonderful, the view from the car park at Haldon was stunning. It was a full moon which lit up the sky. You could see for miles towards Torquay to the west and Exmouth to the east and all the coastline from Dawlish. They agreed that as it sounded like Heaven it must be Devon.

He then drove her home and kissed her goodnight and asked where she would like to go the following night. He insisted on walking her to the front door and didn't leave until she was inside and locked the door behind her.

After that, they met every night. It didn't take Georgina long to give herself willingly to him. She had had a few to drink but that was not the reason. She truly loved him. She found his lovemaking better than with Neil because it was genuine love not lust. The evening was perfect.

Georgina didn't want to take the chance of ruining everything by telling Matt about Neil so she decided to stay quiet about it, after all it would be his word against hers if he decided to drop this bombshell. She stayed quiet - she thought Matt would be devastated.

CHAPTER TWENTY

The next night, when they were in the crowded Smuggler's Inn, she wanted to talk to him but it was so noisy, everyone was there. The Landlord, Len, was on top form, he was standing on the bar singing 'The Music Man' and doing all the actions that went with it. All the customers were following his actions, whether they were drunk or sober. He would always finish the evening by singing 'Von Spiro' when 'Last Orders' were rang, which gave customers ten minutes before the 'Time Gentlemen Please' order was called.

When they got into the car she asked Matt "Do you know of someone who is not very nice looking, about 40 years old and has an anchor and snake tattoo on his right forearm?"

His reply shook her to the core.

He said "Yes, he has been around on and off for some years now, he's called Robert, I don't know where he lives, keeps himself to himself. I thought you knew him because he always asks after you".

"Matt, you must help me with this. We must go somewhere where we cannot be overheard, please help me" she replied, her voice shaking.

When Matt was driving her home, they saw the willowy figure of the ugly man coming out of Lea Mount.

"There he is, I wonder what he has been up to, do you think we should check Lea Mount to see if there is a girl in there?" she asked.

"Hang on Georgina, you can't just go around accusing people of rape – perhaps he has taken a short cut home from the Exeter Inn, or he took a girl in there but she stormed off, just like you did to me when I was walking you home, you left me on the beach, some time ago. Do you remember that?" Matt said.

"Sorry" said Georgina.

CHAPTER TWENTYONE

The ugly man had been watching the young woman for some time. She always walked, to her home, up Teignmouth Hill. This particular night he left the pub before her, he walked up Lea Mount and waited for her in the shadows by the old sentry box. At last, he saw her coming up the hill, she wasn't very fit so was walking quite slowly but was still smoking a cigarette. He let her go by then silently crept up behind her putting his hands around her neck and covering her mouth. She resisted and burnt his hand with the lighted cigarette.

He screamed out "YOU BITCH".

She started to run but his strength was at its peak, so he grabbed her by her hair and dragged her into Lea Mount. She fell over but he continued to drag her cave-man style. He was so dangerously angry, because she had burnt him, that he was full of uncontrollable rage.

He continued to drag her, by her hair, along the concreted pathway in front of the first gun emplacement. He then raped her violently, she started to scream as he was hurting her so much, it was then, in anger, he stabbed her twice in the chest because she would not be quiet.

He continued with his wave of physical dominance towards the young woman regardless of her pain, which was now even worse because of her breathing difficulties due to the stabbing. He didn't seem to care, once again, he seemed to enjoy watching her, it excited him and seemed to make his erection last longer.

After the agonising ordeal for her he left her for dead.

He then made his way to the main road. A car passed him, realising that he had blood on his shirt he quickly went back into Lea Mount and made his way back to the garden along the beach then up the dark Elm Grove Road.

*   *   *   *   *

Georgina and Matt arrived at her Mum's house where they went into the kitchen and Georgina made coffee. She told him the story from the start and showed him Pandy and the jewels. Matt was amazed.

"You must go to the police with this, I will come with you tomorrow, if you like" he said.

"Yes please, and if someone else has been raped at Lea Mount we can tell them who we saw. I do not want to go to Neil Morris, do you think we should go to the Exeter police?" she said indignantly.

After Matt had kissed her goodnight, she wondered if she was doing the right thing in reporting the Ugly Man to the Exeter Police Force. She wondered whether someone would think it odd that she was not going to Neil Morris to report the ugly man coming out of Lea Mount, especially as Matt had been taken into custody as a suspect.

CHAPTER TWENTY TWO

Matt had forgotten that he had promised to take his Mum and Dad to Heathrow Airport in London so Georgina asked him if there would be enough room for her in the car – she fancied a trip to anywhere.

Knowing that Georgina loved Stonehenge so much Matt decided to stop at the site on their return from Heathrow. They walked along with the crowds to the stones and walked around them. They were huge monoliths looking quite majestic in the late afternoon sunshine. They sat on the grass in the middle of the circle in the sunshine and marvelled at the sight, trying to work out how they had managed to form a complete circle all those years ago. After falling asleep for half an hour, they sat and watched the beautiful sunset then headed for home.

As their return to Dawlish was late, they went straight into the Exeter Inn. They walked into the pub, there was no-one there! The Inn seemed strange with no customers. They had walked in through the lower door, nearest the railway station, the empty pub had its usual roaring fire lit in the back corner, the tables and chairs were empty and waiting for drinkers. Ernie was behind the bar, Matt and Georgina sat at the bar by the juke-box which was silent.

"Where is everyone?" asked Matt.

"Everyone is frightened now, we probably won't see anyone now for a few weeks, or until he is caught".

Matt and Georgina said in unison "Who, why, what's going on?"

"Where have you two been all day, there was another rape and murder up Lea Mount last night – she was one of my regular customers, nice girl.

They both seemed to be in shock and both together said "Who?"

"Pam, Pam Edwards" Ernie replied looking downcast.

They all went silent.

The long wooden table by the window had a small bunch of flowers on it and a few beer mats dotted around. Georgina could remember the last time she saw Pam, she was sitting at that long table. It made Georgina feel very sad.

The black and white tiled floor was spotlessly clean and was laid around the corner at the end of the bar towards the small opening that was used as another bar area. It seemed to be really strange when empty.

The door beside the juke-box led to the small inner hallway. It had the main front door leading down the passage to the stairs. The small children's room where Georgina used to sit after the family's Sunday walks was under the stairs. That area had now been incorporated into the 'behind the bar' area.

The inner hallway also led to a small lounge area – this was also empty. Normally it would have been full and buzzing with laughter and chatter. The toilets were across Fishy Lane, the gent's toilet was in the large area that was used as a cellar. The ladies was always kept locked. If you wanted to go to the toilet you had to ask for the key which was kept behind the bar.

The pub was eerily silent, Georgina found it difficult to accept especially as it was normally a very busy, happy little pub.

Eventually, Ernie asked again "Where have you two been all day?"

Matt answered him but couldn't help thinking of Georgina's ugly man that they had seen coming out of Lea Mount last night. Georgina was speechless, she was saddened as she always had a lot of time for Pam.

Beach Street, or locally known as Fishy Lane, stretched from the butchers on the corner opposite the old stables, Edmundo (as he was affectionately called) had his wet fish shop at the bottom of the steps in the thatched cottage opposite the Railway Inn. For a few years there was a jewellers shop between the fish shop and the Exeter Inn that's all there was down the lane.

Ernie kept talking so their discussion about the jewels never took place. Georgina quietly suggested to Matt that they go straight to the police.

"Yes, before we go I will pop home to Mum's that where I left the jewels "said Georgina.

As they were walking down Fishy Lane, two men grabbed them from behind. Georgina saw that Matt was putting up a good fight. Georgina didn't fare that well, she was kicking and trying to bite the man's hand that was covering her mouth, but she found the man's strength too much for her. Suddenly she felt a small prick in her arm and within seconds she could not hear, see or say anything.

When Georgina came round she was lying on a dirt floor, she felt drowsy and had wet herself. Her head felt fuzzy again just like it did the morning after she had slept with the policeman, was she really drugged in that pub?

Georgina could only make out an old, small, dim yellow light at the far end of the room, she could hear sheep, lots of sheep. After a while her eyes gradually got used to the darkness, her night vision was not brilliant but she could see, through her misty eyes, the shape of Matt lying on the floor. Her arms were tied behind her back and her ankles were tied as well so she was limited as to what she could do. The feelings in her head were stopping her from trying to stand up but she managed to shuffle on her backside across the cold dusty floor towards Matt.

"Matt, Matt please wake up. Oh, dear God let him be alive".

She couldn't hear him breathing so she tried to bend over him, she wanted to kiss his bruised and blood-soaked face but an internal pain under her ribs was excruciating. She then tried to loosen the string around her wrists but it was not giving. Her tears started to flow. The only person I know who would do this to us is the ugly man. He knows I have the jewels.

"Matt, I love you, why, when we are so happy, is this happening? It is all my fault, I should have thrown those jewels away a long time ago".

In desperation she managed to turn herself so that her back and arms were close to Matt's hands, as his were tied further up his arms so she was able, after a while, to find his pulse. It was weak and slow, but he was alive!

"Thank God, oh thank God, he is still alive" she said to herself.

Suddenly, she heard a door slam, and just made out the outline of a big man coming towards her, she was very frightened. He was carrying a couple of bottles of water and chucked them towards her. Georgina was so thirsty she felt she could have drunk a bucket of water. Surprisingly, he cut the string around her wrists.

"Where are we?" she said as she was trying to get the circulation back in her hands again.

"Not telling you, the boss will be here soon" he replied in a deep, slow voice that she didn't recognise.

The 'heavy' walked over to the corner of the room where there were some wooden crates strewn around, he piled three of them on top of one another then sank his backside down on them. He found they started to squeak if he wriggled on them, he thought it funny, but in fact it showed how infantile he was.

She started to gently stroke Matts face and hair then tried a little water in his mouth. He came around shortly after that but his speech was very incoherent and he kept slipping back into unconsciousness. She thought they must have given him an extra dose of the drug for him to be out of action a lot longer than her.

"Matt, I am so sorry, it's all my fault, will you ever forgive me?"

There was no reply from him.

She managed to look at her watch, in the dim light she thought it said 1 o'clock. If it was about 9 o'clock when we were abducted, we cannot be very far from Dawlish if it is only 1 o'clock, I have been awake for a good hour now, it must be somewhere local – she was trying to use common sense but was not convincing herself – but which 1 o'clock – morning or afternoon? In this dim light it was difficult to tell and there didn't seem to be any windows.

The 'heavy' in the corner had fallen asleep. Although Georgina could not see him, she heard him snore and she knew she had heard that rattly, heavy snore before – it was Matt's lodger!

'No wonder the ugly man always knew when I was coming home, Matt must have mentioned it to the heavy' she thought.

She managed to doze for a while, then she started hearing the dawn chorus and the sheep, lots of sheep, they hadn't seemed to have stopped all night. Surely we are not in Ashcombe! She noticed that the room had got lighter and realised that some of the corrugated iron roof was missing. She could also see that the walls were cob with ivy scrambling through the hole in the roof. The only place she could think of like this was the old Cider Barn at Ashcombe.

She knew that the old couple that lived in the cottage down the lane were away at their daughters, her old friend Tom Hunt had told her this at the pub last week so it would be an ideal hiding place. Apart from the beaters and guns on shoot days during the winter, probably only the gamekeeper would go up the very steep hill passed the barn, the lane didn't go anywhere. Only the farmer would go into the field, but the entrance to that field was about 50 yards down the steep hill. No-one would be any the wiser, no-one would hear or see anything.

'Dear Tom' she thought 'How lucky he is to have lived in Ashcombe all his life, I wonder what the chances are of him coming up this hill, must be good he always looks so healthy! As he works as a farm hand in the valley, I wonder if he ever brings the sheep to the field up the hill, or perhaps, I can hope, that he walks his dog up here'.

Georgina dozed again, but a heavy boot in her thigh woke her. It was the ugly man.

"Where are the stones, bitch?

"I don't know" she replied, she sounded calm but, really terrified inside".

"If you don't tell me, I will kill you both. Make no mistake, I will kill your boyfriend first, he will have a slow lingering death – and you will watch and then I will take great pleasure in killing you! I have done a stint in Dartmoor for murder so I can quite easily do it again. Think about it".

Georgina was so frightened she couldn't get any words out of her mouth.

He left the barn in a really angry mood leaving the 'heavy' to slam the huge old oak door behind him. From the position where she was sitting she managed to make out the very hilly field across the road from the barn lane and really did think that they were in Ashcombe.

'I wonder if he was the escaped prisoner all those years ago. I really must now dream up a story that he might believe. He appears to be quite clever, but dangerous, almost like a psychopath' thought Georgina.

She gave serious thought to her problem and she came to the conclusion that she definitely must never tell him the true whereabouts of the jewels, because that would be putting her mum in danger, the thought of that was unthinkable.

As her mum lives on her own, it would be easy for someone like him, someone so nasty like him, someone like him who would frighten and threaten her mum, who knew nothing, in his search for the jewels.

She felt she could kick herself for not thinking about this problem before. How could she be so selfish? Surely it was obvious that he would, at some stage, want them back. How could she be so stupid? She has, not only put her mum in danger but, Matt as well.

'Oh, Mum, what have I done? What have I done? Why didn't I talk to you about it, you would have understood and probably laughed at my fear of telling you, just because I should not have gone into the wood all those years ago' she thought.

She felt very guilty and miserable about putting those she loved in such danger. She found it difficult to concentrate, Matt was not coming around as she thought, and had hoped he would, also the pain below her left rib was keeping her from getting in a comfortable position, and the pain was constant.

She decided the best course of action would be not to show any emotion to his threats, certainly not to show that he was intimidating her and she must try to turn his questions back to him. A tall order she thought, especially under duress.

CHAPTER TWENTY THREE

Suddenly the large door at the other end of the barn opened and Georgina managed to get a view of the hedge surrounding the property, she also thought that she had quickly seen the top of the church tower. The door was quickly closed again by the 'heavy'. The ugly man, who was carrying a machete, danced towards Georgina, he was acting completely insane. He was brandishing the weapon, whirling it over his head while dancing and singing 'Oh, what a beautiful morning'.

Georgina was really scared and kept thinking and answering herself 'He is a psychopath I must try to do what I thought of last night.

His dancing continued, but he kept stopping his singing and shouted at Georgina "Where are my stones, bitch?"

Georgina tried to sound calm and just said "I don't know".

"Maybe this will jog your memory". He stopped dancing and lay the cold steel of the machete onto Matt's neck.

"Leave him alone, I told him about the stones only last night. Let him go, please".

"So you have got them, my little lamb" he said.

Georgina realised that he had caught her out. She must be careful what she says to him so she must pacify him rather than be argumentative. She knew she was at a disadvantage, but hoped not for long. She must think up a story but she realised he was quite intelligent so it would have to be a good feasible story.

"I don't know where they are and that is the truth" she repeated.

"No, no, no, no, no, my little lamb. Uncle Bobby is going to get his stones back and you are going to tell me where they are, aren't you my dear?"

He waved the machete over his head again and stood astride Matt, he then brought it crashing down, missing Matt's head by only a couple of inches. Georgina screamed and sobbed.

He then turned to Georgina and said "I have all the time in the world to get the answer I want. I can keep you both hostage for ever if necessary. No-one can hear you. You are alone, completely alone".

He then pointed to Matt and added "He is as good as dead or will be soon. Think about it bitch – all alone with Uncle Bobby and our manservant – what fun we can have!"

He stopped speaking and was looking up at the roof. It was as if he was thinking about what he had just said. The heavy had a stupid smirk on his face. Georgina was sweating and was ready to cry with fear. The beads of perspiration were prominent on her brow. Inside she was trembling and feeling sick.

"Maybe we can have some fun now – just you me and our manservant".

He strode over to where she was sitting, she tried to shuffle away, but he knelt on the floor, grabbed hold of her very sore ankles and pulled her towards him, scratching her bottom on the dirt floor, he then lay on top of her. He was such a weight that she couldn't breathe and her heart was racing. She could smell his body odour and his breath smelt of old ale. His face was very close to hers and she noticed his horrible blood shot eyes staring at her.

"No, no please don't, please leave me alone" she screamed.

She was fighting and trying to scratch his face. He grabbed her wrists then told the heavy to hold her arms. The ugly man moved down her body feeling everywhere, he was taking his time and looking at her face and smiling at her. She was distraught, he made her skin crawl. She screamed and screamed. The heavy easily put both her wrists in one hand and put the other hand over her mouth. She immediately bit his hand very hard nearly severing his little finger, he yelped loudly and let go both of her arms. Georgina was then able to put her arms down either side of her body and then turned her right hand to the floor, picked up a handful of dust and threw it with all the muscle she could muster towards the ugly man's eyes.

This seemed to have worked, he stood up and was reeling around the barn trying to get the dust out of his eyes. He was stumbling very close to Matt, Georgina hoped he wouldn't fall over him – it might make him even more violent.

"YOU BITCH, YOU BITCH" he yelled. "GET ME SOME WATER".

The heavy reached down for the empty water bottle that Georgina had left beside Matt, he rushed out of the door and found an old water butt along the wall.

The ugly man was still squinting and swearing, the heavy came back in and guided him to the butt in the sunshine. Georgina could hear them talking and swearing when trying to get all the grit out of his eyes.

'They are fools to use that old stagnant water, I hope he gets styes, boils and every infection known to man' she thought.

She heard the ugly man shouting really loudly, he was frustrated and it was showing.

"ANOTHER TIME, BITCH" he shouted into the barn.

Georgina could hear the 'heavy' helping the ugly man towards the car and then the engine started and they were gone.

She was so relieved that they had gone then remembered the machete lying on the floor beside Matt and wondered whether she should hide it - but that would aggravate them even more. Eventually she made up her mind she would lay down with Matt and try to hide it under his body. It would be no good to fight them with it – they would win easily.

She was really frightened and hoped they would not come back to rape her. She cried loudly with that thought in her head. She hugged Matt then told him she loved him deeply. Georgina hoped that he could hear her, she hoped that he would regain consciousness and be out of danger. To defend him, would be impossible if she was up against the two of them. She knew the odds were against her.

CHAPTER TWENTY FOUR

They were left alone for what seemed like hours. As she was normally quite a strong person both mentally and physically, she was willing to put up a fight but now that she was so weak she knew she was not capable of even standing on her own, let alone fight. She found a tissue in her pocket and had enough water left to cover the lesion on the side of Matt's face and head. With the machete she cut the string that bound Matt's wrists and ankles she then struggled to get him into the recovery position eventually managing to do it and then felt a lot better. He was still unconscious.

She was able to shuffle around the barn to see if there was any chance of escaping. What were windows were all boarded up, the old cob walls really thick in places with no holes in the walls. Where the 'heavy' had sat earlier, there were large granite stones just strewn about presumably, Georgina thought, from the old cider press. There seemed to be a round granite trough in that same corner that had been just abandoned.

The hole in the roof, where the corrugated iron sheeting had partly come down was much too high to get to and the ivy scrambling through was not long enough – Georgina was much too weak to even contemplate climbing up there!

Not only could she hear the sheep and lambs out in the field, she could also hear the rats and mice scratching around in the barn. Georgina shuddered at the thought of the rats, had they come too close to Matt as he was not moving? She didn't want them anywhere near his open wounds, so she lay beside his body facing him. She could just make out in the murky light his handsome face, his breathing was very quiet. After the attempted rape Georgina was shaken badly, she sobbed for ages still feeling guilty that this mess was all her fault.

She managed to doze on and off throughout the night. Suddenly she heard a car and two doors slamming. The door opened, the ugly man came straight over to her, and his eyes were even more bloodshot than before. She made sure she gave him the impression she was alert and not as frightened as he had hoped.

The heavy was staring at her and kept putting the hand, where she had bitten him, towards his mouth as if he was licking it. It was as if he enjoyed the pain.

"Right, which one first" said the ugly man.

Georgina made sure her voice sounded clear then answered "If you kill him the stones will never be found. I gave them to Matt and he never had the chance to tell me where he had put them, and if you kill me he will NEVER tell you". She carried on speaking "If he doesn't get medical attention soon he will die or be in a coma for the rest of his life. Let me ask him questions – if you stop bullying him he may come around, then you can have your jewels. I don't want the bloody things".

Just the mere thought of someone else having the jewels made him react really badly, he thumped the walls, the old granite machinery and the dirt floor.

Luckily Georgina was lying next to Matt otherwise he may well have started punching him.

"You will never own them – they are mine, all mine he raged. As you are being so stubborn - until you give them to me - I am going to have you! I will rape you every day until you tell me where they are. In fact, my mate over there can have you as well. Think about that!" he said, then started grinning.

"But I have told you I don't know where they are" she yelled.

"I DON'T BELIEVE YOU"! He shouted.

He stormed over to where she was now sitting and thumped her, hitting the left side of her face. The bare knuckle fist smashed into her jaw bone, knocking her senseless, it was as if her brain had reverberated inside her skull. Her face immediately began to swell, closing her eye completely. He had also cut the skin on her jaw bone just below her cheek.

They heard voices coming up the lane, the two men rushed out of the barn and Georgina heard them making excuses to the old couple asking who they should see if they wanted to purchase the barn.

The elderly man in his Devonian accent said "Yer bohy, ee will ave to speak to Major at the Rectory, go down this ere lane, turn left and you'll see the rectory opp'sit the church bohy".

When she heard the ugly man's car going down the lane Georgina tried to scream to get the old couple's attention but she failed, she had no voice she knew they were both partly deaf. By sitting by the old cob wall she suddenly noticed that the men had left in such a rush that they failed to close the heavy door properly.   Even though she still had her ankles bound together, she managed to shuffle her sore bum towards the door, then with the strength that she had left she managed to pull the old door inwards towards her. She was completely exhausted, the sunshine blinded her as she sat outside blinking and letting her eyes get used to the glare of the sun.

There was no sign of the old couple. Georgina was trying to look all around her.

"Yes, we are in the old Cider Barn" she muttered to herself.

Deciding that she must hurry and must get away in case the men come back she realised that she must leave Matt behind. It was an agonising decision but she had to leave him for both their sakes.

She decided to go back to get the machete, then suddenly thought that she could cut through the string binding her legs. The old tool seemed very heavy, so she held it by the hilt and cut the string. Now her ankles, bum and the backs of her upper thighs were really sore. She was obviously not thinking as she normally would – how did she manage to forget to cut through the string? She swore at herself.

She tried to stand and walk but failed. She leant against the wall and shuffled towards the door but was so weak she nearly fell over again. Georgina grabbed the machete, kissed Matt and told him she was going for help. He was still in such a deep sleep that he couldn't hear her.

She found the machete very awkward to carry but was not prepared to leave it behind, the men were too dangerous. She made her way downhill on her backside towards the cottage, every shuffle was so sore and painful she felt as if she was going to faint and the soreness bought tears to her eyes, they were stinging and smarting. Georgina carried the machete on her lap and thought if Ugly came back she would throw it in the hedge. She managed to get to the side of the lane where there was a little bit of grass either side under the hedge, but there were a lot of larger stones that had rolled there when it had rained, so she had to spend time removing the large jagged stones in front of her. Georgina was now sobbing, the skin on her bum and the back of her thighs were so grazed they were bleeding and now full of dirt and dust.

She tried to stand again, but her legs just would not hold her weight, she collapsed forward so she stayed on her hands and knees and did find it a bit easier to crawl down the steep hill. She held the machete by the hilt again and pushed the stones away in front of her.

It took Georgina ages to get to the cottage, there didn't seem to be anyone around so she carried on to the stream, her favourite beige coloured mini kilt was now in tatters. She lay and leant over the edge of the stream then lifted the water with two hands and felt the coolness of the water glide over her face and hair after drinking heavily.

Suddenly she heard a friendly, familiar voice.

"Hello maid, bloody hell what's going on?"

Georgina recognised the voice, it was Tom Hunt with his dog. He looked shocked to see her in this state and realised she desperately needed help.

She tried to speak but couldn't, in a slurred voice she just said "Matt barn".

Tom looked shocked "Did Matt do this to you?" he said.

Georgina realised he had misinterpreted what she said and started shaking her head. Even that easy movement of her head she found was painful.

She started to write in the dirt that was beside the stream 'MATT BARN' and was pointing to the Cider Barn. Underneath she wrote 'COMA'.

"Who has done this to you?" asked Tom.

She then drew an anchor with a snake coiling around it. Tom immediately knew who she meant. He had seen him loads of times in the Exeter Inn. Tom thought he was a bit strange because he was very quiet and didn't offer any insight into where he came from or where he lived, he avoided any questions as to his past. Tom was a bright young man, he was not the type to have the wool pulled over his eyes and he was quick to suss people out, but where this Robert was concerned Tom could not get to the mysteries of his life, but he felt sure there were lots to hide.

Tom also had agreed with Matt and the other local lads when chatting in the Exeter Inn that the policeman from London was such a cocky character that he was not liked or even believed.

Tom wanted to ask Georgina lots of questions but said "Your Mum is very worried, she couldn't get hold of Matt's parents because they are abroad, and with the recent murders in the town, she has gone to the police".

Before rubbing out the anchor, she wrote beside it ' killer rapist'. She then wrote again 'amb, police'.

Tom tied his dog to a low growing branch, his dog was now quite elderly, and so Tom started to run alone to the telephone box. Georgina knew that he would not let her down, he would get an ambulance if it was the last thing he ever did. She just had the strength to hide herself behind a fallen tree trunk in case the men came back. They would surely kill her now. But what about Matt! She didn't have the strength to get back up the hill, in fact she didn't have the strength to do anything.

The tree trunk completely hid her from the road and the dirt lane, she laid down on the bumpy but soft grass. She could feel the warmth of the sun on her face and body and could smell the wild late spring flowers – she thought she was in Heaven. Her thoughts took her back to the mid-fifties, the happy days when life was just a big holiday. For a young child living in Dawlish nothing was rushed, nothing was serious, everything was just perfect - until the ugly man came along!

Her body wanted to rest but her brain was telling her to stay alert. She watched the lambs gambolling in the orchard but weakness was beginning to take over. Her eyes felt droopy and she had a buzzing sound inside her head, it was as if she had been injected again.

She tried to keep her brain alert by working out what day it was. She couldn't. She even had trouble remembering what month it was. The lambs are out, primroses were dead, the bluebells are in full bloom as was the wild parsley and the Hemlock so I think it must be April or May she told herself. The apple blossom is not quite out yet so it must be May. She then heard a cuckoo and remembered the old saying that Tom had told her:-

'The cuckoo comes in April,

Sings his song in May,

In June he sings another tune,

Then in July he flies away.

She then tried to imagine her and Matt getting married, buying a little house together, sitting in front of a large roaring fire, with a large map that Matt had bought in Exeter, planning a trip of a lifetime together every evening instead of watching the television. The heat from the sun on her face made her dreams seem like reality. In her head she was now in Greece, walking up towards the Parthenon.

Georgina thought she could hear a bell ringing. She was beginning to drift off but the bell was getting louder as it was coming up the valley.

Tom came running back, he was not even out of breath, his face red due to the heat from the sun rather than the half mile he had just run. All Georgina could do was cry, she tried to spluttered out about Matt in the barn, but felt that she had been to the dentist and had 10 injections in her mouth and plenty of gas as well. Georgina was so exhausted she could barely breathe let alone tell the story of the stones. She didn't care anymore about her mother telling her off for going into the wood. She didn't care anymore about whether she would be accepted as a Civil Servant with a police record. All she could think of was Matt.

Tom said "I am going up to see if Matt is ok then I will go to the lane and flag down the ambulance and police. Matt will be ok I am sure".

When he came back, Tom was not even puffed out, he told her he thought Matt was still unconscious, she could only whisper the story out, she hoped that Tom understood what she was saying, but he couldn't it was too garbled.

"I cannot understand you, maid", he said alarmingly.

Georgina found another patch of soft earth and wrote. 'Jewels in Pandy.'

"Bloody hell maid, what jewels and who or what is Pandy?" said Tom. He was so shocked to think all this could happen in Dawlish and Ashcombe. Only lately did things happen in Dawlish and not much happens in Ashcombe not to this extent. Rape, murder, prisoners, jewels – this sounds like a film script!

Georgina was so exhausted and relieved that she was free and that someone else knew the story, she couldn't say anymore.

She lay on her right side as her backside was so sore and her back was resting up against the old tree trunk. The pain in her left side was excruciating and her ankles were throbbing where the string had dug into her ankles. She tried to remember what organ was on her left side, was it her spleen or one of her kidneys? She should know but couldn't remember. The sunshine should have been a tonic but she was past that. Dreams of Morocco, India and Africa were filling her head, and making her wanting to live, but she was feeling like death.

In her head she tried to sing the old hymn that Matt used to sing to her, but she could only think of a few words. She hummed the tune, closed her eyes and drifted off into oblivion.

CHAPTER TWENTY FIVE

Georgina opened her eyes, she could hear a beep, beep, beep noise coming from the machine next to her. She could see a white ceiling and a clock above the door, which said twenty to one. The second hand seemed to go very slow. She was in pain, her right foot was knocking the end of the bed and her mouth was exceptionally dry. She realised she was in hospital when she recognised the blanket that was covering her very sore body.

"Hello, how do you feel?" said a voice from the side of the bed.

It was a pretty young nurse who spoke very quietly. When she smiled her teeth gleamed a gorgeous bright white almost as white as her starched cotton apron. The nurse held a small sponge filled with water to Georgina's lips which tasted wonderful to her.

"That's enough for now, we don't want you to be sick, do we?" Said State Registered Nurse Karen Lovell.

While Karen continued to take the readings from the machines then checked Georgina's temperature and blood pressure, a Doctor entered the room. He also asked how she felt.

Georgina managed to say "OK".

The nice young doctor checked the reading on the machine and looked at the progress chart that the nurses had kept at the foot of the bed. He read the reports that were in the manila coloured file that was on the table.

"You are doing very well, get some rest and I will come back later to see how you are getting on".

The doctor's bedside manner was excellent so Georgina felt she was in good hands and settled back and slept for some time. She didn't know what was wrong with her but thought, no doubt they would tell her later.

After several hours the doctor came back with an older gentleman and a couple of nurses.

"Hello Georgina, my name is Mr James Cooper, I am the Senior Gastroenterologist and this is Doctor Brian Williams, also a Gastroenterologist. When your mother visited she gave permission to operate on your spleen, which had been badly damaged, luckily we have managed to repair this organ. Can you tell me how that happened?"

Georgina had trouble remembering anything, the only memory that came to mind was Matt. She had come out of her anaesthetic induced sleep with him on her mind.

"How is Matt?" she asked.

The specialist replied "He is as well as can be expected, you can see him soon. Now please tell me how you received your very bad injuries".

"We were beaten and injected with something then held prisoners in an old barn in Ashcombe. Matt was taking a long time to come around from this, I did manage to put him into the recovery position and kept talking to him, but I never had a response, is he going to die?" asked Georgina.

Georgina could feel the tears rolling down her cheeks, the doctors saw this as well, it was all too much for her, not seeing Matt was like being tortured all over again.

"Please do not upset yourself, we will come back when you are feeling a little stronger. Try to think what was inflicted on him. It may help his recovery" said Mr Cooper.

"Why do you ask me these questions, while I was being beaten Matt was being beaten as well, I did not see what they did to him".

"The police will want to question you, but I will not allow this to happen until we are sure that you can cope with these traumatic questions, but you can still have visits from your mother, brother and sisters, but only two at a time".

"Thank you Mr Cooper, before you go can I ask when I will be allowed to visit Matt?"

"Not for quite a while Georgina, he is still a very poorly man" he replied.

Every time a nurse came into the room she would ask after Matt.

"How is he" she pleaded.

Very often she would get the reply that didn't tell her anything. 'I don't know' or 'He is on another ward' or 'I will find out for you'. Then she wouldn't see those nurses again. She found that really annoying which made her angry and thought she was going crazy.

It was another three days before Karen was on duty again. She displayed sympathy to Georgina's plight and when asked about Matt she said she would phone the other ward and find out. At those kind words Georgina started to feel a little happier.

The next day Nurse Karen returned with the news that Matt was comfortable but still in a coma.

Mr Cooper came to her bedside shortly after she received the news about Matt and once again asked her how she felt.

She replied "I will not feel better until I have spoken to Matt".

"But, he is still in a coma, I fear he will not hear you, Georgina".

"Please let me try".

"I am not sure it would benefit either of you" he said.

"But if we don't try, there is no hope is there" snapped Georgina.

The weeks went by then out of the blue, Karen entered her room and told Georgina that she could visit Matt for just a few minutes.

"Oh, that's wonderful. Can we go now?"

"Slow down Georgina, I have to unplug you from this machine and put you on a mobile machine, and we have to get your dressing gown on".

"Can you put a comb through my hair?" asked the impatient Georgina.

"Georgina, please remember that Matt is still in a coma. He is still very poorly.

"I know, I know, I hope he still remembers me".

Georgina found transferring from the bed to the wheelchair very painful, but she made no sound as she was worried they would not allow her to make this visit to his bedside. Karen brushed her hair and helped her to get her dressing gown on that her mother had bought her. She was so excited.

Karen thought it would be good for Georgina to see different people in the lift and along the corridors of the hospital, but Georgina didn't really take much notice of them, her mind was fixed on visions of Matt. Suddenly she was there, outside his room, her heart was pounding to see the love of her life again after all this time.

Karen pushed the wheelchair to his bedside, the venetian blinds were pulled down covering the window so shading the room from the morning sun. Georgina could still make out his handsome face, he was sleeping peacefully - she desperately wanted for him to wake up. Holding his hand gave her comfort. Georgina squeezed his hand in the hope that he would clutch her hand back, but he didn't.

"I love you dearly Matt, please wake up. I know it is all my fault. Oh Matt I am so sorry, so very sorry, please forgive me".

Georgina started to sob, it was all too much for her.

"We must leave him to rest now" said Karen as she turned the wheelchair around and out of the door.

Georgina couldn't remember the journey back to her side room. When Karen managed to get her back into bed she tried to sleep but couldn't. She was awake most of the night worrying about Matt and her nightmare during the last days of their imprisonment was starting to come back to her so every time she opened her eyes, instead of visions of Matt's handsome face, she just saw the ugly man staring at her.

The next day Mr Cooper did his rounds and Georgina was told that, probably her visit to Matt did do some good, he had come out of his coma but was still very poorly.

"Mr Cooper, is Matt going to be OK? How long will it take before he is back to normal? What exactly are his injuries?" She was pestering Mr Cooper for these answers.

"I am sorry Georgina, I cannot give you any information because you are not next of kin. You must ask his parents. At the moment he must rest and have no visitors. I also have to tell you that the Police are asking me when you will be ready to answer questions regarding your kidnap, do you think you are ready for that?"

"Yes, I suppose so".

*   *   *   *   *

Georgina's family were allowed to visit her the next day and she was delighted to see them. Her mother, her two sisters and her sister-in-law all travelled to Exeter on the bus. They bought lots of goodies to eat, spare nighties, soap, toothpaste, deodorant and shampoo. It was so good to see them.

Her elder sister offered to wash her hair, but she wasn't bothered, not if she couldn't see Matt.

In between tears she managed to apologise to her mum and said "I am so sorry to have caused you all this trouble, please forgive me".

Her mother replied "Don't worry about it, it's all over now, just concentrate on getting better. Do you know how Matt is? I tried to phone his mum but the telephone was a bit funny and I kept getting cut off - I hope it was the line and not her".

Georgina quickly thought that it was not over, she still had the stones in Pandy!

She really didn't want to think about them at the moment so she started to tell what she knew about Matt's condition.

"I was able to visit him, can't remember which day, he was still in a coma then but luckily he came out of it soon after. The doctors won't let me visit him now, he is too poorly and they won't tell me how he is because I am not next of kin".

Georgina's family tried to cheer her up by telling her the news from Dawlish.

Her mother took up the story that the policeman from London went to see her regarding a 'Mr Pandy' who they wanted to question, the family thought that was so funny they were rolling about laughing. Mother continued by saying that this Neil, the DI from London, was a cocky young chap, he also gave Mother the impression that he was devious and she wouldn't trust him, so she made out she didn't know anything about Mr Pandy.

"Honestly, if that is the best the Met can offer, then God help us all" announced Mother. "Tom Hunt often phones to find out how you are. He told me he thought you said something about, what sounded like Pandy, but your speech was so slurred that he wondered whether he had misheard you".

Georgina didn't want to add to their worries so she laughed it off and said she couldn't even remember talking to Tom.

"Well" said her mother "If it wasn't for Tom, you and Matt would probably be dead. I thought this policeman was a bit thick, I didn't like him. He is an insult to the Devon Constabulary. Good job your dad isn't here".

Her sisters then joined in with the rest of the news. Apparently, they said, that according to the Dawlish drums Matt's lodger has been arrested and charged with kidnap, seems like he was working on his own because there didn't seem to be any one else arrested.

'That's odd', thought Georgina 'I wonder how the police came to that conclusion. The quicker Matt and I get well and go home the better and I promise, for Matt's sake, to find the ugly man and see justice done. I will work towards that'.

Georgina started to remember the policeman, Neil from London, and how he tricked and drugged her in Brighton. She shuddered to think that she lost her virginity to him – her treasured virginity that she was saving for Matt.

CHAPTER TWENTY SIX

Within a couple of days, two policemen came to take Georgina's statement, luckily Neil Morris was not one of them. She was pleased about that. She did her very best to remember everything about their capture and imprisonment in the old barn, the beatings that her and Matt took, the attempted rape, her escape and Tom Hunt finding her and calling the police and ambulance.

They did ask a lot of questions and Georgina was tiring fast, but she was adamant that she should tell whatever she could remember. She also told them that she saw the ugly man coming out of Lea Mount about 10.30pm the night Pam Smith was murdered.

What she did not reveal was the reason for the abduction – the jewels.

The day arrived when Georgina was allowed home but this tired her more than she ever thought it would. Phoning the hospital every day to find out about Matt kept her from going completely mad, although the nurses on the ward never really said anything just that he was 'doing well'. It took some time before Georgina realised that this was a 'run of the mill' answer to someone who was not next of kin.

Three months later Georgina asked when she could visit only to be told 'it could be another month' she was upset about this. That time scale made her feel very down, her mother insisted that she rested but Georgina found this very

boring. If she slept during the day, she couldn't sleep at night and if she didn't

sleep during the day she found she would have horrendous nightmares of the

ugly man which kept her awake at night.

Eventually the day came when she could visit. She was over the moon

with joy. She went to the shops and bought him fruit, orange squash, a

magazine and chocolate, she knew he loved a chocolate bar.

Her bruised face had gone from black to mauve to pink, then green and

yellow and back to her normal olive skin. She had managed to cover other areas

with a thick cloggy foundation and with her lipstick on she managed to look

presentable.

Georgina caught the bus from the Catholic Church to Exeter then walked

to the hospital. The large red brick building in Southernhay had stood for a

century or more and was still regarded as the best in the west. She went inside,

it was crowded and approached his ward with trepidation – it was almost as if

she was frightened of seeing him. She was so happy as she was led to a small

side room but the shock of seeing him was almost too much to bear. He was sat

in a chair, he was dribbling as the nurse was feeding him. He didn't recognise

her in any way, his eyes, his beautiful brown eyes, were empty and sad. He still

had wires and tubes coming from him that fed into a large machine on his right

hand side. Once again, she vowed there and then to find ugly and bring him to

justice.

Almost immediately, the door opened and in walked Mr and Mrs Thackeray. She seemed to sneer at Georgina and went directly to Matt and kissed him on the forehead. A small piece of meat was stuck to his chin so she wiped it away with the bib that was around his neck.

"How are you Georgina?" Asked Mrs Thackeray.

"Getting there" Georgina replied cautiously.

"Good for you" Matt's mum replied nastily. "Look what you have done to our lovely son".

Matt's dad tried to calm her down but she was having none of it.

"Now, now, it wasn't Georgina's fault and you know it" he stated.

"Oh yes it was, why involve my son in your sordid little life?"

"He wanted to help me. He didn't know anything until the day we were kidnapped"

"Well, your chance has gone now, when Matt is discharged from here we will be taking him to convalesce so that he can be happy away from you, where he can recover completely. So I am telling you to leave him alone".

Georgina bent over and kissed Matt on the forehead and walked out of the room. She didn't dare reply to his mum because she felt she would burst into tears and probably say something she may regret.

Walking down the corridor the tears were streaming down her face, to make matters worse she was sobbing by the time she reached the bus stop.

'How could she be so cruel, she doesn't know if Matt still loves me' she thought.

Another month went by and Georgina decided to visit him again. Every time she phoned the hospital she was fobbed off with the same old phrases as before. She would see for herself how he was.

The bus was full of Christmas shoppers heading for Exeter. Georgina couldn't muster any enthusiasm for the festive holiday or the New Year, which was Matt's favourite party time. 'What fun they had had last Christmas' she thought.

She walked down the, now very familiar, corridor only to be told by the nurse sitting at the desk that Matt had been discharged and his parents had taken him for convalescence. The hospital were unable to tell her where. Georgina was devastated. Without Matt in her life, she was nothing.

Her mother came home from shopping the next day and told her that she had heard on the Dawlish Drums that Matt's Mum and Dad had taken him to North Devon.

Georgina quickly packed a small bag and arrived at the railway station just in time to catch the train to Bideford. A small B&B was opposite the station so she booked a single room for a week. It was a friendly little place and, with the help of the owners, she managed to find a Convalescent Home in Northam that Matt was booked in to.

Unfortunately, every time Georgina went to visit she could see Mr and Mrs Thackeray through the window. She spent one evening in the B&B writing to Matt, telling him she still loved him and was looking forward to the day when they could be in each other's arms. She delivered the letter the next day, but hadn't thought about the fact that Matt was now unable to read, so the letter was given to Matt's mum.

Georgina soon ran out of money and decided that, because it appeared that he was being well looked after, his mum being so anti Georgina, she would go home and wait for him.

Her mother told her to get a job, mainly because she thought it was in her best interest mentally. She also said that Georgina needed to cheer up and maybe go out with her friends. To pass the time, one cold wintry day, Georgina decided to look at the jewels still in Pandy. They were just as bright as they ever were when she found them. She put them back into the soft stuffing of the old cuddly toy and promised herself to do something with them along with bringing ugly to justice.

She had plenty of time to think of a plan which she managed to do but kept it to herself. She knew her mother would disapprove and still no-one knew about the jewels. Tom Hunt thought he had misheard and probably told the police that. Mother had not had a visit from the Detective for nearly twelve months.

As spring was approaching, the Dawlish Drums were spreading rumours again and Georgina's mum heard that Matt and his mum and dad, had moved back to Dawlish. Georgina felt so happy she thought it would be so much easier to see him.

Apparently the drums said that he was walking and talking now but was a little slow at thinking. Georgina was just delighted that he was home.

Unfortunately, her happy dreams came crashing down when an announcement appeared in the local rag that Matt had married a girl from North Devon. Georgina was once again left feeling completely heartbroken.

CHAPTER TWENTY SEVEN

All Georgina wanted to do was to go to bed and stay there. Her mother was beginning to worry about her mental state. She would lay, wide awake, trying to think, just trying to get some answers as to why Matt had married someone else. In her thoughts he was always going to marry her! The mental visions of Matt and this new woman together made her so miserable.

She decided to think about where it all went so wrong – and immediately came up with the answer - the jewels!

'That's where it all went wrong, all those years ago, when I first saw that ugly man and then when I found the jewels. I wish I knew where he lived'.

Another voice in her head reminded her that she would never find out where he was or where he was hiding while she lay in her bed.

'You must get out of this pit you are lying in and take action, go out into the world and hunt him down, then you can accuse him of all the damage that he has done to you and Matt. Where is this nasty thug of a man, is he still in Dawlish or has he gone back to wherever he came from?' she said to herself.

That thought reminded her of the old gamekeeper at Ashcombe, he would always say, in his strong Devonian accent, "Us 'ave seen 'em come and us 'ave seen 'em go, maid".

'But I don't think ugly has moved away, he will stay here until he gets the jewels back' thought Georgina.

Thinking she would have a busy time soon when she got a job, she got up from her bed, had a shower then told her mum she would go to the Department of Employment and Productivity at Teignmouth to enquire about vacancies in an office. Her mother was relieved and pleased that, maybe, she was coming out of this awful minor bout of depression.

The government office in Teignmouth was small and friendly, they advised her that they had just been notified of a vacancy for a secretary needed in a bank in Exeter. That, she thought, would suit her fine.

She made her way to Exeter by bus straight away. The interview went well and, was told that, providing the references were good she would have the job within a month. Georgina was both pleased and grateful – she really needed to money.

On the journey home, she was able to think quietly and decided to pay a visit to that cad Neil Morris to see how much further he had got with his investigation regarding their kidnap.

She made her way to the temporary Incident Room at the Manor House where the Desk Sergeant informed her that there were no further leads as to the capture of the rapist or the murderer. Unfortunately, he also could not give her any further information regarding the kidnap.

"Can I speak to DI Neil Morris please?" a very irate Georgina blurted out.

Just at that moment, Neil, looking anxious and tired, walked in through the front door. He had heard Georgina's request and just beckoned to her to follow him into his office.

Georgina had planned on being very cool and clever towards Neil, so after closing the door behind her, but before she could say anything, she found that he had taken the reins in the conversation as soon as they were alone.

"What a lovely surprise, Georgina, it is so nice to see you, how are you and Matt? I understand he got married while he was away in North Devon. That's a lovely area and the girls are really nice up there as well" he said with a well-intentioned smirk on his face.

"Tried them all have you?" said Georgina sarcastically then tried to continue in that 'put him down' vein.

"I have come here today, as you are the reputed Officer-in-Charge, to ask what you have found out regarding our captors".

"Not a lot and not a lot I can discuss" was his curt reply.

"Why is that?" she replied.

"We haven't an awful lot to go on, but we are following, hopefully, another avenue that has just been passed to us. That is what I cannot discuss with you. You do understand, don't you? By the way, can you tell me where I can find this Mr Pandy? No one seems to know him. You did tell Tom Hunt that, didn't you? Is Tom Hunt friendly with the man you call Ugly?"

"No, of course not" she quickly replied. "Tom has nothing to do with this".

"Are you sure, it seems that he arrived on the scene almost immediately after your escape from the barn. I want the truth from you Georgina. You don't want the good people of Dawlish to know about that night in Brighton, when we were in bed and you tried to corrupt me with helping you to sell some jewels, do you?" He lied.

What are you talking about? Why are you saying things like that?"

"Come to my flat tonight, I already have a bottle of gin in the cupboard waiting for you, we could have some more fun".

Georgina was horrified, she felt that she could have died of shame. How could she have been so stupid to think that he would help her? She ran out of his office and made her way quickly up Stockton Hill.

She had the chance to think some more as she puffed her way up the very steep one in four hill and quietly wished had never come back from London. She thought 'If I had some spare money I would go back to London to visit my old friends'. Then an idea popped into her head – she would telephone Brenda, her friend she had worked with. Brenda's husband was in the Met and had been for years, maybe he knows of him. Brenda was also easy to speak to and would take a secret to her grave.

Meanwhile, Georgina vowed she will not have anything more to do with Neil again, certainly will not be seen in his company and will never be left alone with him.

Georgina phoned Brenda that evening. It was nice to speak to her friend again after all this time. She was anxious to tell Brenda about the rapes and murders in the town, but not about the kidnap, that would wait for another day.

"I did read about this in the national newspapers some time ago. I was in shock to think that that was happening in your lovely little town. I did speak to your mum but you were out with your new boyfriend. Come on, tell me all about him, he sounds really nice" said Brenda.

"It's really a long story Brenda, I will tell you everything one day. First I must ask you about the Detective Inspector, he is called Neil Morris, and I understand he comes from the Met. Has your Alan come across him?" Georgina asked.

"Oh no, is that where he is, we did wonder where he had gone, poor you and poor Dawlish. He is a nasty piece of work, the men here found him to be a liar and would get anybody into trouble just so that he could climb the ladder. They also thought that he was 'in' with a criminal gang, although he kept saying he was trying to get information. He may have fooled the top brass but he certainly didn't fool the older coppers, but they could get no proof of his activities. He was too clever and always covered his tracks well. He did move quite quickly, now that you have told me he is a Detective Inspector that says it all!"

"I don't understand, what does it say?" said Georgina.

"Well it says that, as he is very young for that position and because he was not liked at the Met, he was probably given the promotion so that he could be moved on. Don't trust him Georgina at all". Brenda replied. "Must go now, baby's crying. I will phone you next week to find out about this new boyfriend of yours. Take care".

Georgina tried to think like a policeman. She prayed to her dear father in the hope that he would guide her from above. She would search her seaside town until she dropped but knew she needed to be careful as she was now on her own. How she missed Matt, his calming influence on her, his gentle touch and the way he spoke in that deep sexy voice. Everything about him she missed.

'Don't get maudlin' thought Georgina scolding herself.

The next day she got up with the sun and decided to walk the dog along the beach. It was a lovely spring day, a bit chilly but dry. There were only a few early morning walkers at Coastguards beach. It was quiet and Georgina walked in the newly washed sand, she kept her head down as her eyes were scouring the wet sand as she looked for treasure that, maybe, had been washed up while she was beach combing.

She took her eyes off the sand when she noticed at the top of the beach, her mum's dog, Judy, was being shooed away by a tall man who was wrapped up with a scarf which nearly covered all of his face.

Judy was continuously barking, unfortunately, the more she barked the angrier the man was getting.

'No it cannot be, surely that is not Ugly. How can he so blatantly walk along the beach, picking up firewood, when he has done so many horrible things in this town'.

Judy obviously wanted him to throw one of his sticks for her to chase and was taking no notice of anything else. Georgina didn't want to shout to the dog in case Ugly recognised her voice, so she whistled not knowing whether Judy would even hear the shrill sound let alone obey and come running back to her.

Georgina decided to stay back and already had made up her mind to follow him. Now was her chance. The ugly man was determined to shake off the aggressive barking of this pesky dog. Eventually Judy came back and she managed to put her on the lead. By this time Ugly had managed to walk off the beach and was heading for Coastguards Bridge. Georgina was concerned about going over this bridge because at the top of the many steps on the other side, the path that ran alongside Mount Mariah could not be seen from the beach, the bridge or the road. Luckily a man walking his black Labrador walked up the steps so Georgina followed him closely, she then felt safer.

The black Labrador called Bertie was very interested in Judy, so much so that his owner had no chance of moving forward until Judy was walking beside him. This Georgina was really pleased about. They followed the ugly man, without him realising, to the top of the cliff then crossed the road and reached Elm Grove Road within minutes. The walker and Bertie then carried on down the Exeter Road which left Georgina to go on her own.

The dustmen were walking slowly beside the dustcart, Georgina knew all of them as they were all Dawlish born and bred men.

"Morning Bill, morning all" she said.

"Morning maid" they all replied with a cheery smile.

Georgina wanted to go faster because of the stench coming from the open top dust cart and managed to rush past easily. She caught sight of Ugly again when she walked under the conker trees and saw him turn into Oak Park Road by the post box.
Within the little time that it took her to run the 50 yards to the bottom of the private road, he had disappeared completely.

She thought the only place he could have gone in that time was into the first Villa – unless he was hiding behind some bushes in the Villa's large garden.

'Did he see me following' she thought.

She knew the people that owned that Villa and he certainly wasn't one of them. Georgina decided to sit on the branch of the big tree to see if he came out of hiding, so she tied Judy to the smaller lower branch and climbed the tree.

The junction where the post box was cemented into the wall was where it started all those years ago. A shudder went through Georgina's body and her mind was starting to relay all those thoughts and nightmares she had had to endure. After a while, she could smell the dust cart coming up Elm Grove Road. She thought it best to go home, the dustmen would certainly think it odd that she was sat on the branch of the old fir tree.

The only way off this branch was to either jump or climb down. Georgina decided on the latter. As she stood up, she found she was now tall enough to look over the rooves in the old walled garden. What she saw very nearly made her lose her balance and fall. There heading towards the greenhouse, chatting casually and laughing was the ugly man and DI Neil Morris.

She was in a state of shock, she never, ever thought that that would happen. Georgina partly climbed and partly fell down the tree. Judy was excited because she thought she was going to continue her walk. Georgina managed to avoid landing on top of the dog but fell onto the rough gravel between the road and the tree. She thought she was lucky that she had only grazed her hands, lower arms and knees.

Georgina was shaking with worry and her grazes were now bleeding by the time she had reached the front door. She could hardly believe what she had just seen and felt really anxious that the ugly man was so near to her home. She also wondered how long Neil Morris had known the ugly man's whereabouts and been in contact with him.

'Oh Matt, my darling Matt, please come back to me soon and save me from this hell. I miss you so much and I cannot live without you' she thought.

CHAPTER TWENTY EIGHT

The next day Georgina's mum came home from her doctor's appointment and mentioned that she had seen Matt in the waiting room.

"He looked well and was walking and talking much more easily now. He did ask after you and told me that he misses you. He also walks over to Coryton Cove every day at 2 o'clock. I don't know why he said that, maybe he said it for a reason" she said with a grin.

Georgina replied with a twinkle in her eye "I think I might go to the beach hut this afternoon, just to check on it after the high winds last night".

Her mother winked, how happy she would be if they were to be married.

The beach hut was at the back of the cove by the wall and was on stilts. The winds were still relentless which kept a lot of people away from that part of the beach. Georgina managed to open the locks easily and checked inside, everything was in its place so she pushed the bolt back to lock the bottom doors, she kept the top stable door in the upright position then put the kettle on.

A few minutes later she saw, through the windswept sand, the outline of her lover coming towards the beach hut. He was nearly doubled over as he battled against the wind. Georgina's heart was pounding as he came closer - his still very handsome face, his eyes nearly shut and his hair full of very fine sand that had been blown by the south westerlies.

He reached the bottom of the wooden steps and she welcomed him with open arms. Neither of them spoke they didn't need to, the joy of being together at long last and the love they had for each other just made everything disappear into another world. They collapsed in each other's arms and made passionate love on the floor of the hut.

As they lay cuddled together Matt told her he was not happy. His wife had returned to North Devon and they were talking of divorce. Although she was saddened to think that he had to go through this trauma, Georgina was secretly delighted.

"I really must tell you the latest turn of events. DI Neil Morris is not to be trusted, he is in cahoots with Ugly and, according to an old friend of mine in London, Brenda, I have told you about her, she is married to an officer in the Metropolitan Police Force, Neil Morris is bent. Also he is trying to put all the blame onto Tom Hunt. He really is a horrible little liar" she said.

"We will visit Brenda and her husband, if you like, he should be able to advise us. We can take the jewels with us as evidence" he replied.

Georgina felt as if the weight of the world had been lifted from her shoulders.

'I knew he would know what to do, he is as reliable as ever'.

It didn't take long before they fell asleep. Georgina woke to the sound of the wind, which was now howling much stronger, the curtain had been blowing outside and it had got dark. No wonder she felt cold. She looked at Matt's face and thought he looked as if he hadn't a care in the world. Covering him with the old picnic blankets she thought how lucky she was to have such a thoughtful lover.

In the cupboard under the primus stove she found a bottle of gin and some orange squash. She managed to find some glasses and handed one to Matt when he woke from his slumber.

She looked at the man in the moon and thanked him for being so kind.

"Don't be so stupid, Georgina, and this is before you have had a drink! I still love you, you know, we will get all this sorted out, I promise.

"And I love you too, Matt".

They giggled together, it seemed like a million years ago that they managed that. They were so happy.

The wind had dropped when they awoke early next day. Georgina found her washbag in the cupboard and took her pick from the many towels in the drawer, then she put the kettle on.

"I am going around to Boat Cove for a wash, the fishermen would have opened the toilets by now, won't be long" she said as she kissed him lovingly.

While she had gone Matt found the coffee and prepared two cups then wrapped the blanket around him and sat, in the sunshine, on the wooden steps outside the beach hut. He heard the scream of a Peregrine Falcon and was watching the gulls ducking and diving and trying to frighten the bird of prey away from their nests.

He shuddered a few times, not through the chilly early morning but he had a funny feeling that he was being watched. It was an eerie feeling and he worried about Georgina. He quickly rummaged through the old chest of drawers and found the pair of binoculars that were kept there. He ran down the sand and just managed to get a glimpse of the Ugly man and Neil Morris making their way up Lea Mount. They started to lean over the railings and were looking at Georgina coming back from the ladies toilets. She waved to Matt not knowing she was being watched. They fell into each other's arms and kissed passionately.

He managed to keep her looking towards the railway tunnel so that she could not see the two men. He didn't want to alarm her.

"Let's go to London for a couple of days, we can visit your friend and take the jewels with us. We won't tell anyone except your mum. There is a train about 10 o'clock this morning. Let's just go and get this sorted once and for all".

CHAPTER TWENTY NINE

Matt paid for the two rail tickets, they then boarded the 10.15am train to Paddington, he was looking at everyone on the platform and anyone that got on the train with them at Dawlish station. If they were being followed he didn't want to be looking over his shoulder for the next couple of days. All of the people who did get onto the train were Dawlish people so he knew they would be safe.

The five hour journey was pleasant and every time they stopped at a station Matt was looking again at everyone who boarded the train. Georgina thought maybe he was being over cautious but that was better than someone following them.

They arrived at the hotel that Matt had selected. It was clean and friendly but crucially it was in central London and within easy distance to Scotland Yard and her friend Brenda's house.

Georgina insisted that they rest for a while after phoning her friend, they were to meet up in the evening at Brenda and Alan's house, Georgina was looking forward to seeing her friend again. Matt had already got into bed and was dozing as Georgina lay beside him. He stirred and they spoke of how much better they both felt that the Metropolitan Police Force were, hopefully, going to close this awful chapter of their lives that they had endured for the past few years.

As Georgina lay in his arms, her recollection of their nightmare started to come back to her. She could see, in her dreams, the jewels that she had found when she was a young girl, the Ugly man's face when he was trying to rape her and the inside of the barn where they were held captive. She woke with a shudder. Hopefully it will be all over by tomorrow she thought.

After showering they made their way to the Embankment and walked beside the river which was still a busy area in the dying light of the evening.

"Are you 100% sure that these friends can be trusted?" Matt asked.

"Yes, of course. Alan has been in the Met for years" Georgina replied.

"So was Neil Morris, or he said he was. Do you remember him telling us that down the Exeter Inn one night? I am sorry Georgina, but I find nowadays I cannot put too much trust in anyone, except you, of course" said Matt smiling.

They arrived at the house quicker than they originally thought and found Brenda about to take the children upstairs to bed. Georgina was amazed how they had grown and was pleased to be able to meet the baby at last.

Alan was busy in the kitchen putting the final touches to the curry that he had cooked from scratch and he was ready to pour drinks as soon as they had arrived.

The house was large and homely, Matt liked it and said it was a house built to be filled with children and added that he wanted one just like it. They sat at the table which was laid beautifully and set for four.

Brenda had given Alan a rough idea of what and who they wanted to talk about and he started the conversation by saying that he was not a bit surprised by the actions of Neil Morris.

"Nothing surprises me about him, my colleagues and I knew he was a cheat, but we could never get to the truth to be able to do anything about him. I wouldn't trust him at all. He will stop at nothing to get what he wants" said Alan strongly.

When Brenda came down the stairs, Alan put a glass of gin and orange in her hand then showed us to our places at the table, Georgina started by showing the jewels to Alan and Brenda – they were amazed at the size of them.

"This puts a new slant on things, those jewels must be worth a fortune, no wonder this man you call Ugly wants them back! With the murders and rapes in the town we should work fast. The best bit of your story is that you saw this man, coming away from the crime scene you call Lea Mount - were there any other witnesses?" Alan asked.

"We haven't heard of anyone and living in Dawlish we would have known the next day if there were, I can assure you" replied Matt.

It was about 10.30pm and a few glasses of gin later before Matt and Georgina left their friends house. As they were leaving Alan promised to speak to his senior officer and arrange a meeting, hopefully the next day. Matt and Georgina were really pleased with this initial outcome and got into the taxi, that

Brenda had organised, feeling a lot happier.

They both slept a lot better than they had for a long time feeling sure that the course of action they had taken was the right one.

Alan phoned the hotel the next day before10.00am, as promised, to let them know that an appointment had been made for them to see two high ranking officers at Scotland Yard at 12 noon that day.

Superintendent Danny Fryer, a huge man with a big cheery welcoming smile and an equally pleasant, slimmed down version of his boss, Chief Inspector Sam Andrews were already sat at the massive sized table in the sparsely furnished Board Room at Scotland Yard. They made Matt and Georgina feel at ease instantly. Alan, who accompanied them already knew his superiors and had previously told the anxious pair from Devon that these men were the best there was in the British Isles. This information did wonders for Georgina and Matt's confidence in people.

"Welcome both of you to Scotland Yard, I understand you have a story to tell, would you start right back to the beginning. We will ask you questions when you have finished" said Superintendent Fryer.

Georgina started to relate the whole story right back to Ugly flashing to her, the jewels that she saw him bury in the wood, then when she took the jewels and had hidden them in Pandy, and the reason why she hid them, the anchor and snake tattoo on his right forearm, the times that they had seen him in the Exeter Inn and the number of rapes and murders that had happened in the town.

I will stop you there for a moment, perhaps you would like some coffee and a rest for five minutes" said the Chief Inspector.

Georgina excused herself and asked where the Ladies toilets were while her coffee was cooling down. She had found the story telling exhausting but she knew she had worse to come.

The meeting continued in the Board Room when Matt came back from the Gents toilets.

Georgina continued to tell the story truthfully, as much as she could recall, about the night they were kidnapped which was also the night after the, hopefully, final murder.

Matt interrupted by saying "From then on I knew nothing until I woke up in hospital four months later".

Georgina blinked back the tears as she told them about the fear and cruelty they had instilled upon them both mentally and physically in the old rustic barn. She also mentioned about Matt's lodger being a friend of Ugly and how they tried to rape her but she fought back and finished up being punched in the face by Uglys fist. She continued by telling them of her escape from the barn and being found by their old friend Tom Hunt who was walking his dog.

"It must be nearly time for a cup of tea" said Sam Andrews, "Let's take another short break".

"Good idea" said the Superintendent. "I had already organised tea and cake, I will have it delivered right away".

When they resumed the meeting, Georgina continued with the information they had found out since their hospitalisation. The fact that Matt's lodger had been arrested but, most crucially, that Georgina now knows where the ugly man lives and the horrifying knowledge that DI Neil Morris is friendly with him and that Morris was trying to put the blame onto Tom Hunt!

When Georgina had finished blurting that out she burst into tears mainly through the frustration of not being able to stop Morris.

Superintendent Fryer intervened and asked where the jewels were now, so Matt took them from his inside jacket pocket and handed them to him.

"Wow, look at the size of these jewels, I will give you a receipt for these and we will endeavour to find the owners – although that could prove quite difficult, but there could be a reward for these" said Fryer.

He decided to call it a day and suggested they have a good night's sleep and resume tomorrow at 10am.

It was 8pm when they returned to the hotel after finding a restaurant, where they had an excellent meal and a couple of drinks. They both collapsed in a hot bath and were in bed by 9.30pm and slept till 7am.

* * * *

Back in the Board Room at Scotland Yard the next day, they were quickly joined by Danny Fryer and Sam Andrews again. Today they were told, was going to be like an inquiry - Georgina and Matt were ready for it.

Matt was taken into an office across the corridor and Georgina stayed where she was. They were given large books of photographs and asked whether they could see Ugly in these albums.

It was while Matt was looking through the second tome that he spotted Ugly and told Sam Andrews, who was with him. The book was taken away and put on the top pile for Georgina to look at next. She could hardly lift the book, it was quite heavy and when she came to the picture of Ugly she froze. It was definitely him, the horrible large eyes, and the close lipped mealy mouth. It was definitely him and she said so to the Superintendent.

When Matt came back into the room, they started to ask a lot of questions and were asking for dates. Georgina could only say that she first saw Ugly when she was about seven or eight.

"Can you tell me his address, Georgina" said Sam Andrews.

"Um, no, I don't think there is one. It is a walled garden that presumably would have been originally owned by the large house, now a hotel, at the top of Oak Park Road.

Sam Andrews continued "Do you know where the jewels came from?"

"No, I don't, oh dear, I am not being very helpful am I" she said.

"Don't think like that Georgina, you are doing really well" he replied.

After lunch the meeting resumed and Matt immediately asked if their answers had been useful, because Georgina was feeling a bit dejected owing to the fact that she couldn't answer all of the questions.

Danny Fryer answered "Yes, you have both been very helpful. We can now tell you that the man you call Ugly, is in fact called Robert May and he escaped from Dartmoor Prison in December 1954 after serving only a few years of a life sentence for murder. The jewels you gave us were from a collection that was stolen from the Nazis in 1945 when allied troops stormed Berlin. It was originally suggested that a soldier, either British or American stole them then sold them to a gem dealer in London, they were then stolen again in a raid that hit the headlines in every newspaper in Great Britain. It was a robbery with violence, the poor night watchman received horrendous injuries – just like you Matt. It was this jeweller, who had bought them in good faith that reported them stolen. That was in 1955 and it seems that you have had them ever since and I can now tell you they are worth a fortune!"

He continued "Whether Robert May had anything to do with the robbery is yet to be established, if he did, he will never be released from his next prison. With you both and the good people of Dawlish, we now consider this a very delicate and dangerous situation, especially where you and your families are concerned, we would suggest that you do not go back to Dawlish until they are both, I mean Robert May and Neil Morris, are in police custody. We can help you to re-locate temporarily or give you police protection. I would advise re-locating."

"I cannot leave my mum on her own and the family in danger" Georgina blurted out. "We must return to Dawlish!"

Matt agreed with her and added "My parents could be targeted as well and if we do not go back to Dawlish, I am sure Neil Morris will realise that we are missing."

"He won't be in Dawlish for much longer, as soon as we have hard proof, we will call him to come to London to up-date us regarding the murders, which is normal practise. Meanwhile, while Morris is here we will meet with the Devon force and recapture Robert May. Does he know where you live?

"I don't know but Neil Morris certainly does" answered Georgina.

"Go back to Dawlish and try to stay at home as much as possible, especially at night. Are you back to work yet Matt?"

"Unfortunately, no, not yet" Matt replied.

"Well, your excuse for your absence from the town, if asked, could be that you just do not feel like going out, especially in this horrible weather. Years of experience have taught me to arrange things as naturally as possible. We will of course, arrange for a team of plain clothes policemen to shadow your every move. These are very experienced men who will watch over you at all times, but you will not know they are there."

Georgina and Matt both said "Thank you" at the same time.

"Now go home, do not tell anyone about your shadows and we will keep in touch. Cheerio both of you, please stop worrying, we will fix it all" said Danny.

Brenda's husband, Alan, was waiting in an adjoining office, he rose to greet them when he heard them walking down the corridor,

"Well now, feel better?" he asked.

"Yes, much better, take care and when this is all over please bring Brenda and your children down to Devon, we must keep in touch and thank you for all your help" said a very grateful Matt.

They walked back to the hotel after stopping at Trafalgar Square and finding a quaint little pub where they enjoyed a drink to, hopefully, celebrate the ending of their nightmares.

CHAPTER THIRTY

After telling the events of the last week to her mum, they agreed that it would be best to stay indoors, as advised, until the police told them it was safe to go out.

"We have enough food to last us ages and your sisters can get anything we need when they go to work" said her mum.

Georgina knew that her mum would cope with this situation very well. She had always been resourceful and strong – typical of mothers that had gone through a war and brought up children when their menfolk were abroad fighting.

The days, for Georgina, were drifting into each other. Evenings were passable with the help of the television but it was filling the days that were the boring times for her. Knitting, sewing and jigsaw puzzles were not holding her attention due to her constant fear and worry about Matt and his family. At night she double checked that the windows were closed and the external doors bolted and secure.

Although surrounded by houses, Newlands was within the beautiful Devon countryside and all the creatures that belonged in it. So it was not surprising that the awful human-like scream of a dog fox, the grunting of the hedgehogs and the many screech owls, which were all part of country life, didn't scare Georgina and her mother at all. What scared them was the thought of Ugly and Neil Morris breaking into the house looking for the jewels even though they had the knowledge of their 'guardian angels' from the Met looking after them.

Two of these men had been watching the 'secret garden' from behind the shrubs and bushes at the front of the first villa in Oak Park Road. After a couple of days, at about 6.30am, the Ugly man and Neil Morris, who had met on the beach, went into the secret garden through the small wooden door. Once inside, the police were able to move position and stood on the branch of the big old fir tree. They were then able to take a number of photos of the pair together showing full facial shots, undeniably a true record of Neil Morris and Robert May.

Within a couple of days, Neil Morris had been summoned to Scotland Yard for an update on the rapes, murders and kidnapping that had happened in Dawlish. Once there he was questioned relentlessly. He had an answer for everything and denied all knowledge of Robert May and blamed Tom Hunt for the kidnapping. It was only when shown the photographs of him with May in the garden that he eventually admitted knowing him.

He was arrested and held in custody and, after his meeting with a solicitor, he was given a date to appear in court.

The next morning, the ugly man was listening to a play on the wireless when he heard an unusual noise in the garden. He went outside his 'living hut' and found ten or more uniformed police officers in the garden. He was surrounded and outnumbered in strength - he knew he was beaten. The plain clothed policeman from London started to arrest him for the murders of the Prison Warder, the young girl at the bus stop, the lady in the Manor grounds, the murder of Pam Edwards in Lea Mount and the kidnapping and assault of Matt Thackery and Georgina Cartwright and the attempted rape of Georgina Cartwright. The ugly man interrupted, in a loud voice, by declaring that he was not Robert May but Anthony Davis.

"I have my Birth Certificate to prove it, look in the tin in the bottom drawer beside the bed" he raged.

A police officer found the tin and took it with him to the police car that was parked in Elm Grove Road. Ugly, who at this time, was shouting, swearing and proclaiming his innocence at the top of his voice, had been handcuffed and bundled into another police car and was taken to Exeter Police Station for questioning and, after a lengthy interrogation, was held in a cell until an officer came from London to question him regarding the jewels.

It was another week before Danny Fryer and Sam Andrews, from the Met, first called at Mr and Mrs Thackeray's house to inform them that it was now safe for them to go about their business and to ask Matt to come with them to Georgina's mother's house. Mrs Thackeray was against this until Matt told her that she must accept Georgina or lose him. He didn't want to speak so harshly but Georgina was the girl he loved and nothing would stand in his way.

His dad interrupted "Leave it to me bohy, I will talk her round".

"Thanks Dad".

They arrived at the house at Newlands, Georgina was so relieved to think that it was, at last, all over and that she was in Matt's arms again. She started to cry then sob then laugh – her emotions were everywhere. It was just the sheer joy that the nightmare had come to an end – she could hardly believe it. Georgina's mother made tea for everyone and then Danny Fryer began to tell the story of the arrests of Robert May, Neil Morris and Matt's lodger.

They had decided that a Police Award would be given to Tom Hunt for his bravery when he found Georgina. His actions probably had saved her and Matt's lives. This was considered very heroic to stay with Georgina, when she and Matt were unable to defend themselves, and he would have been, like them, in a very dangerous situation had the two kidnappers came back to kill them.

While they digested all of this new information the Met officers finished with handing Georgina an envelope. She opened it slowly, she had no idea what was inside. To her surprise it was a cheque, with a very large amount of money written on it from the Insurance Company rewarding her for the return of the jewels!

"Oh Matt, there is enough money here to buy a cottage and go travelling around the world. Let's go, it is the answer to our dreams, I love you so much".

"I love you too, maid" Matt said as he put his arm around her and pulled her closer to him.

Georgina's mum, however, although very pleased with this outcome, had serious doubts as to whether the police were right to give Matt and Georgina, maybe false hopes that all was well. She had thought long and hard regarding the identity of the ugly man. If he is who he says he is, and has a birth certificate to prove it – and no images of fingerprints were found in the Prisoner 1852 file at Dartmoor Prison, then he was not the ex-prisoner who killed the prison warder at Dartmoor Prison. The police had no evidence at all that it was Robert May or Anthony Davies who murdered the three girls whose bodies were found in Dawlish. Which makes it obvious that, although a difficult pill to swallow, Neil Morris was, it appeared, just trying to do his job - without success!

Only the ugly man knew that the old gardener was still lying in an un-consecrated grave at the bottom of the 'secret' garden. He chuckled to himself as he lay on his temporary prison bed in Exeter Prison that he had stayed one step ahead for nearly 20 years!

THE END